CLARA BERGE

Alexa

Published by Seraph Creative

Alexa - Clara Berge
First Edition, 2020

Copyright © 2020 MJH van der Spuy
United States / United Kingdom / South Africa / Australia

Published by Seraph Creative in 2020
www.seraphcreative.org

ISBN: 978-1-922428-14-1

eBook ISBN: 978-1-922428-15-8

Typesetting, Layout & Cover by Feline www.felinegraphics.com

Dedication

I want to thank Yeshua for opening the veil between earth and heaven. You made it possible for us to have true peace, Your peace on earth.

I want to thank the Spirit of wisdom and understanding for helping me write what Yahweh had laid on my heart to write. Thank you for the scrolls.

I want to thank the angels and heavenly host who helped me in more ways than I can imagine.

Special thank you to Lindi Masters, you are an amazing inspiration. I'm so honoured to have you in my life.

Also thank you to Dr. Yana Sanders for sharing your wealth of revelation of the Hebrew language with me.

Thank you to Ian Clayton for pressing into the revelation of nanotechnology and the kingdom to make a way for us all to follow.

All the special people at Seraph Creative, you are a blessing to me. Thank you for helping me bring this story to the world and for designing the awesome cover.

Finally, thank you to my family and friends. You are my cheerleaders and I could not do it without you. For every encouraging word and every read-through, thank you. I love doing life with you.

Foreword

I have known the author for 15 years and have seen her blossom into a wonderful mother, wife and now, writer.

Ever since I met her, she has been enamoured with books, creating art and wanting to write. I think it is in her DNA.

Her writing helps us to put into stories, some of life's mysteries which help us to perhaps understand them on a more personal level.

She has always been one who pursues the mysteries of the "unseen" and "invisible" world.

It's something we have often spoken about. The how and where and the possibilities of these mysteries and the "unseen", being made tangible in our lifetime.

The story of Alexa is intriguing, spanning the past and the future and making it manifest in the present encompassing technologies we are beginning to see in our day and age. What a journey!

What an enjoyable read, that I am sure you will find intriguing.

Lindi Masters
House of Masters Ltd
Ignite Hubs International

This story is for the broken,

For those who long for peace.

May you find Him who gives rest to the weary

And strength to the weak.

Luke 1:79

To give light to them that sit in darkness and in the shadow of death, to guide our feet into the way of peace.

Romans 8:6

For to be carnally minded is death, but to be spiritually minded is life and peace.

1 Peter 3: 10-11

For he who would love life and see good days, let him refrain his tongue from evil, and his lips from speaking deceit. Let him turn away from evil and do good: Let him seek peace and pursue it.

CHAPTER 1

The thirteen-year old boy crouched beside his mother who lay on the filthy mattress in the corner. Her long black hair lay tangled across her face, knotted and unkempt. She lay on her stomach, one arm hanging off the mattress.

He moved her hair back. She used to be beautiful, before the drugs and the men. Stories about their life before his father died sounded like a fairy-tale. He couldn't remember much himself. His father died trying to right a wrong by interrupting a street robbery.

The boy prodded his mother's shoulder to make sure his suspicion was correct. The clammy coldness of her skin confirmed it. He imagined her united with his father and felt relieved for her. He rubbed his fist against his chest, his face contorting for a moment.

Getting up, he gathered everything that had any value, which wasn't much and left without a backwards glance. Time for him to start living his own life. As he stepped into the warm humidity of Mexico City, he pulled back

his shoulders and held his head high. Silently he vowed that he would do better than his father.

He wouldn't just right one wrong. He'd right all the wrongs.

James stood still as the metal gate clanged shut behind him. His somber gray eyes scanned the enclosed space. The room was bare and boasted only a small single bed attached to the floor and two shelves bolted to the right wall. A desk chair would've been nice. He started lifting his hand to move his fringe to the side before remembering they'd shaved off his blond tresses. He grimaced.

Casually he sauntered over to the bed and climbed under the covering, turning his face to the wall. The thin gray blanket lay against his cheek, the coarse material prickled. Pretending to scratch his left ear, he pressed his lobe twice.

"James, is that you?" The woman's voice was slightly breathless.

"Yes."

"I'm so relieved, you've been quiet for weeks." She cleared her throat. "We've moved into the new house. Alexa is doing well."

"Any problems?" He pulled his head deeper under the blanket, speaking into the pillow.

"No. We're fine." There was a hesitation in her manner.

"Everything still set for next month?"

"Yes, as far as I know." She fiddled with the pen on the table, her heart beating erratically.

"Great." James gave a slight sigh.

"Do you miss us, I mean the group?" She fell silent, looking downwards, clenching the pen in her fist.

James stayed silent for a minute longer until she thought he had gone before his melodious voice floated through the speaker.

"Yes. I miss you."

A red blush spread up her neck to her white freckled cheeks.

"Bye, Ruth, take care of her."

"I will. Take care of yourself too."

She stared at the quiet speaker, reaching out to finger the silver metal for a second, so near, yet so far. Involuntarily she shivered. Doubts like nasty little bloodsuckers were attached to her, distracting her from her task.

Shaking her head, she took a few deep breaths. The front door opened and her face lit up. "Welcome home, Alexa. How was your day?"

Oscar squinted up at the girl in consternation. From his position on the concrete floor of the basketball court with the sun behind her, she seemed for a moment otherworldly. He put his pride in his pocket and took her hand. It took no effort for her to lift him. The snickering of the other children registered. He felt himself blush, his almost transparent skin, tinted red.

"Thanks. I could've gotten up myself."

He stared at his tattered trainers, seeing the blood running down from his damaged knees to his white socks. His stomach felt rock hard.

"Who's your girlfriend, Oscar?" The jeering voice of the gang leader that made his life hell in school sounded right next to him.

Oscar jammed his hands into his armpits. More fuel for their fire.

"I'm Alexa and I don't know Oscar. Why are you treating him so disrespectfully?"

The cool, modulated tones from the girl in front of him startled Oscar. He focused on her only to find himself staring into blue eyes that seemed brighter than any eyes he'd ever seen.

"What, your name is Alexa? Did your parents name you after a virtual assistant?" John, the gang leader, sneered. His crewcut black hair and dark eyes made him look even more intimidating.

The girl did not seem riled at all. "Maybe. You haven't answered my question."

John was the tallest in their class and he now towered over the girl, as he stepped nearer to her. "I'm the leader around here, Alexa, Lexi, girl. So, if I decide I don't like someone, that's my business. And I don't like new girls that put their noses where they don't belong. Oscar here is a freak. An albino, and an African American outcast, who shouldn't grace the same school as us. Choose; will it be him or us?

She stared at him almost without blinking. "You are rejecting him based on his outside appearance. Something he had no choice over. That does not seem fair."

"Don't worry about it. I'll be fine." He had meant to say that in a confident voice, but it came out with a tremor.

Alexa looked at him; her face broke out in a smile. "I like you." Turning to John she said. "I choose the fair way. I'm on Oscar's side."

John pushed out his chest and punched his fist into the palm of his other hand, hissing, "You're going to regret it."

The bell rang, and the gang dispersed, leaving Oscar and Alexa alone on the playground.

He wanted to tell her to sod off, scared for the trouble she would be in because of him, but he felt her hand on his shoulder.

"Two are better than one, don't you think?"

A weird sensation started in his stomach and he beamed at her, which she answered with a smile of her own. Together they rushed into the school and she chose a seat next to him in the class.

It dawned on him that Alexa was the most beautiful girl who had ever spoken to him, never mind sat next to him. Her hair was blonde, tied up in a neat ponytail, matching her blue eyes and light skin. Everything about her just seemed perfect. When the teacher started asking questions, he discovered that not only was she pretty, she was clever too. There wasn't anything she couldn't answer.

Someone threw them a scrunched-up paper from behind. He opened it up and read the black letters saying: "You're both dead."

She glanced at it but didn't look afraid. Just smiled and threw the paper in the bin.

The worst part of his day was when he waited for the bus down the street to get home. Usually, he timed it so that he only had to leave the school with a few minutes to spare. Today, Alexa stayed next to him as he hovered inside the hallway. He was bouncing his curled knuckle against his mouth, his eyes flicking back and forth from the clock on the wall to the door.

"Do you live far away?" Alexa softly asked.

"No, but I take the bus, it's safer. I live in Beaumont Drive." He pulled at the straps of his backpack before putting his hands in his pockets.

"That's near to my house, I'm in Greenside." She grinned at him.

"Oh, wow, just one street up from me." His forehead was sweating, his stomach churning.

"Do you want to walk? I estimate it would take us half an hour. Fresh air would be good."

"I'm not sure I know the way."

"I do."

He wiped his hand across his forehead, bit his lip and then blurted out, "But it's not safe. If John spots us, he will follow us. Him and his gang."

Alexa shook her head, "I'm not afraid. You will be perfectly safe with me."

Her confidence seemed to rub off onto him, although his knees still bore the evidence of the breaktime scuffle. "We can try."

They walked past the bus stop, where the other kids were congregated. Oscar could feel the menace of John's stare on his back as they hurried past. Keeping his head down, he itched to run. He didn't dare look back.

After a few minutes, Alexa whispered, "They are following. Five of them."

He felt his heart sink like lead. "You should run, it's me they want."

"Two is better than one, remember." She winked at him.

"Alexa, I don't want you to be hurt."

She sighed. "Let's turn in here."

He followed her only to find himself go ice-cold; she'd turned into a deserted side road. She swivelled around and waited for their pursuers.

"Are you crazy?" His breath burst out of him in short gasps. He felt dizzy, his legs and knees were turning into water.

"Please stand a few meters away from me, block your ears and promise you won't tell anyone what you saw today." She implored as the boys advanced towards their position.

John was the first to harass her, "Told you we were going to make you sorry for choosing his side."

"This is your last warning. Leave us alone and you won't get hurt." Alexa's voice had a quiet steel in it that made the hair on Oscar's arms stand upright. He placed his fingers in his ears shifting a few meters away just like she asked. She threw her white jumper's hood over her head.

"Do you believe this girl, boys? She thinks she can take on all of us?" The other boys jeered, but her behaviour seemed to unsettle them.

John took another step closer to her and tried to grab her arm. The next few moments felt as if they happened in slow motion. Oscar watched with wide eyes, as John grabbed his ears, instead of her arm, with an outcry of pain. All five of the boys seemed to suddenly be in acute agony which forced them to their knees. She took out her phone and took a picture of them before whispering something in John's ear, which made him go pale. Beckoning to Oscar, she left them there in the street.

Once they were around the corner, Oscar had found his voice again, "What did you do to them? Wow, that was amazing! Why did you take a photo? What did you say to John! Do you have superpowers? Wow, wow, wow!" He was bouncing up and down and waving his arms.

Alexa chuckled at his exuberance. "Slow down. No, I don't, well, in a way, but not really. I can't tell you how I did it, but it's enough that they won't be a problem anymore. If they try something, I'll post the photo embarrassing them in front of the whole school."

The reality of what she did for him started sinking in. He

placed his hand on his heart, there was a lightness in his chest. "Alexa, thank you. Those guys made my life hell. I'll do anything for you, anything at all. You have a slave for life."

She nudged him on the shoulder, "I'll settle for a friend. I don't have many of those."

"Why not? You're amazing!" His cheeks tinted red again as he realised what he said.

She shrugged, "We've moved around a lot. It is hard to fit in when you are different."

"Tell me about it. I've not had a lot of friends either although I've stayed in Queens all my life."

The man with the long gray jacket slowed his steps. The teenagers didn't notice him. He'd made sure he kept a long way behind them as he trailed them from the school. When they'd gone into the side street, he'd positioned himself out of sight, but near enough to observe what they did.

Interestingly, the girl could do something ordinary people couldn't. It confirmed the other stories he'd heard. He turned away, backing around to his car. He already knew her address and everything else there was to know about her and her mom. It didn't surprise him to trace a connection to the notorious hacker JJ who was incarcerated at present.

Arriving at his base of operations, he parked his car a block away in a large car park. The nondescript building stood tall amongst other tall buildings. There was a concealed back entrance that he used, ignoring the front doors. Its upper floors housed offices, but a hidden elevator took him down to the basement under the proper basement. There were ten people working in cubicles in the large room. He strode to the corner where his right-hand man sat.

"Hi Mole."

The large guy, squatted in front of a setup any gamer would drool over, swivelled around to face him. His eyes were magnified behind his glasses. Along with his baldness and the appearance of no neck, he did faintly represent a mole.

"What happened?"

"I'm not sure. I followed her on her way back from school and she did something that brought a few boys harassing her to their knees."

"Did she have something in her hand?"

"Nothing that I could see. It looked like she generated it herself."

"Holy moly. Seriously?"

The gray coat man sat down at his own desk behind Mole's elaborate set-up. "There's something going on, that's for sure." He sat still, gazing at his blank screen.

"What do you think?" Mole scratched behind his ear.

The other man fixed him with a stare, "We will have to watch closely. I want to review everything we know about James and Ruth Johnson and everyone associated with them in the past."

"Whoop! I love the thrill of a challenge." Mole's face stretched into a Cheshire cat's grin and he rubbed his pudgy hands together.

The gray coat man, whose name was Sean, didn't smile. He started typing his report in detail. This might hold a lot more complications than first thought.

They reached her street first. Oscar noticed that there weren't any trees on the sidewalk and

both sides of the road were flanked by detached single-story houses. Each wooden framed house had its own unfenced small garden in front, and a garage on the left side which mirrored the street he lived in. He walked her to her house, which was number thirteen.

Oscar scratched his head, "Do you know, I think my house borders on yours at the back. I recognize that tree."

Her brown front door opened and a woman with dark auburn hair and blue eyes, the same color as Alexa's, came out.

"Hi Alexa, who's your friend?"

"This is Oscar, Mom. Oscar, my mom, Ruth."

"Pleased to meet you, Ma'am." He stretched out his hand and she shook it.

"Pleased to meet you too, Oscar."

"We think his garden borders onto ours, Mom. Can we check it out?"

"Sure, afterwards come inside for some cookies and juice." She let them enter and they dropped their backpacks in the kitchen before going out the back. Alexa stood the ladder up against the concrete fence, and they found they were looking into Oscar's tidy back yard.

"What a coincidence, hey?" Oscar said.

"Yes. Do you need to let your parents know where you are?"

"No, they both work late, I take care of myself in the

afternoons. I'm an only child." His voice sounded wistful.

They packed the ladder away and went in through the backdoor. The kitchen had a breakfast island separating it from the lounge. The yellow curtains with white daisies gave it a cheerful feeling. On the island, Alexa's mom had placed two glasses of apple juice and a plate full of home-baked apple cinnamon cookies. They sat down on the high bar stools and helped themselves. Oscar took a whiff of the baked goods, wondering if it would be impolite to take more than two.

Alexa's mum came in and leaned against the sink. "How did you meet?"

"We are in the same class." Alexa made it sound simple.

It was on his lips to tell of how she helped him with the bullies, but she gave a slight shake of her head and instead, he said, "Alexa was sitting next to me and we discovered we live in the same area, so we walked home together."

Ruth smiled, "That's nice. We only moved in here last week so making new friends is at the top of our list."

"His house is behind ours, Mom. Would you mind if we used the ladder again, so he could just go home over the fence?"

Ruth's eyebrows lifted, "Sure if his parents won't mind."

"They work late, I'm sure they'd be all right with it." Oscar gave her a shy smile.

As they walked towards the fence later, Alexa looked up into the large oak tree in Oscar's backyard. "Do you have a treehouse?"

"No. I've always wanted one, but my dad's never had the time to build one. I guess I'm too old for one now." He pressed his lips slightly together.

"I've always wanted one too. Maybe we could build one ourselves? We shouldn't give up on our dreams just because we've reached the grand old age of fourteen, should we?" Alexa held her head up, her shoulders straight. She quirked an eyebrow and smiled at him.

Oscar eyed his tree, "Well, I've got planks that I've saved up over the years, and my dad has all kinds of equipment in his shed. We could give it a go if you want. " He scratched behind his ear.

"I'll draw up a plan for us and we can start this Saturday." Her eyes sparkled and he grinned.

"I can't wait." With that, he climbed up on the ladder and slid down the other side.

That night as he lay in bed, he felt like a different boy from the one who woke up that morning. Instead of dreading school, he couldn't wait to go, to see Alexa again. How and why she wanted to be friends with him eluded him, but he was so grateful that she did.

His insides felt all warm and relaxed. "Thank you, Father. Thank you for Alexa. Please bless her." With that, he fell asleep.

In her own bedroom, Alexa smiled as she heard his softly spoken prayer. In fact, she had heard his sobs as he implored God to help him the previous night. It felt weird that he thought she was an answer to his prayer, which in a way she was, although God had nothing to do with it. She turned over on her side staring into the darkness. If a being like that existed, she wondered if he would help her if she needed it. With what she was planning to do there were multiple things that could go wrong.

All that separated the bustling streets of Chongqing from the interior of the coffee shop was a thin pane of glass that rattled every time a larger vehicle sped by. The man perched at the tiny two-seater table sipped his steaming cup slowly.

This break was his one daily luxury. Twenty minutes was all he afforded himself. His mobile phone beeped, causing a frown on his broad forehead. The hand that picked up the phone showed the lines of his age and he pulled his hand back instead of checking the message. It was overworking that made him look older.

Most men in their fifties started pacing themselves, getting ready for a slower pace of life. To him, however, it felt as if his life was only beginning. Life a month from now would look completely different.

For the first time, he smiled as he drained his cup.

If only his father could see him now. His "weak" scientific son who'd overthrow all the militaries and governments of the world. He wished him alive just so he could tell him "I told you so." He thrust out his chest, before settling back in the chair, a warmth radiating throughout his body.

At least it would be satisfying to bring an end to the perpetual bureaucracy that stood in the way of his research. After this he could experiment on people as much as he liked. One of the first things he'd do was make himself look young again. He could envision his new look already. He studied the lines on his hand again before lifting his head. Time to stop daydreaming and get to work. He stood and crossed the three meters to the till.

"Xiéxié." He thanked the girl behind the counter, placing his cup down on it. Stepping out on the sidewalk, he held his hands lightly behind his back and blended in with the crowd until he was only one among many.

The first Saturday morning in March dawned clear and sunny although it wasn't warm. Oscar counted the hours until their agreed time of ten o'clock. He'd pulled out all the planks and spread them out across the yard. They needed to be treated otherwise their treehouse wouldn't last long. He felt her shadow fall over him and looked up with a smile.

"I didn't hear you come over."

She gave him a quiet smile before finding a paintbrush for herself. They were both dressed in old jeans and jumpers. Alexa's hair was tied back in a ponytail. A companionable silence filled the air while they worked. After a while, Alexa started humming. The tune wasn't happy or melancholy, it was simply comforting. As Oscar listened it felt as if all the cells in his body responded to it, absorbing the sound like an energy drink.

His wristwatch soon showed it was past lunchtime and he knew by the rumble in his stomach they needed a break.

"My mom left us lunch in the fridge. Come on."

He wrapped his paintbrush carefully in plastic wrap to keep it wet. Alexa did the same. The kinks in his back were complaining and he stretched his hands high, rolling his neck. Good thing he'd applied sunscreen and got a hat on that morning. Even early spring sunshine could burn his skin.

They fetched their lunch and sat down under the shadow of the oak tree. There was a salad and egg and mayonnaise sandwiches with a bottle of lemonade.

Oscar licked off his finger after satisfying his hunger with two sandwiches and a few mouthfuls of salad. "I had a strange dream last night."

Alexa tilted her head, "Tell me about it."

Oscar fingered the small silver cross he carried around his neck. "I dreamed that I was attending your wedding."

Alexa's lips puckered in a smile. "Who was I marrying?"

"A tall man with blond hair. You were both young, early twenties I'd say. "

Alexa gave him a blank look.

He lifted up both his pale hands, "Hey, I didn't make it up. You had a beautiful bouquet of pink and red roses. Your mom was there and someone else, I think your dad."

She pushed her hair behind her ear and pinned him with a stare, "Did you watch a movie lately with a wedding in?"

"No. I don't watch romantic mumbo jumbo." Oscar rolled his eyes. "That's why I said it was a strange dream. Normally my dreams are all over the place, but this one felt real, like an experience I've had or will have."

A shake of her head, "All things have a scientific reason behind them."

"Really? Says who." He lay down on his stomach, his feet up in the air, chin resting on his hand.

She followed suit, across from him. "I don't want to argue with you."

"Just humour me." A smile played on his face, his almost transparent skin wrinkling around his eyes.

She rolled her eyes, "I've looked into all the weird and wonderful things people believe are supernatural and most of the time they are not."

"So how do you explain our existence."

She was quiet, her eyes examining the grass intently. "I don't. None of the theories can be proven."

"Uhuh...You won't get it 'til you let Him show you."

"So, you think you were born this way by design? With a higher divine purpose in mind?" Her voice was curious, without any judgement.

He rolled over onto his back, gazing up through the bright green leaves to the blue sky above.

"Don't think I haven't asked why a million times. It doesn't seem fair. But then in the grander scheme of things you could say I'm blessed to be this way."

She kept quiet, intent on hearing his line of reasoning.

"I've been spared the trap of believing that outer appearance defines who I am. I value and work at the inner parts of me while at the same time loving the body that serves me. And the list goes on..."

"Yet if you could be normal, you'd choose that?" Alexa sat up, tucking her knees against her.

"Maybe, but if my being different drives me to discover the true meaning of life, wouldn't it be more of a blessing than a curse?" He inclined his head watching her digest what he said.

"Tell me how you imagine a world of peace looks like?" She dipped her head sideways.

Without hesitation, Oscar replied, "A world where everyone loves their neighbour as themselves."

Alexa's eyebrows lifted. "Interesting." She stood up

and held out her hand to pull him up, "I like your way of thinking."

The sun had dried their planks and they got down to measuring and cutting them to the right sizes. It was a simple design, with a sturdy floor and ladder, three walls with a window at the back. For the roof, they had found two sheets of transparent plastic. As the sun was setting, they drilled in the last screw. Together they packed away the equipment and then, as excited as two younger kids, climbed up into their handmade shelter.

They sat cross-legged in silence, listening to the creak of the tree and the rustle of the leaves.

Alexa's eyes seemed brighter even though dusk was falling fast. "I love it."

Oscar grinned at her, "Me too."

"I didn't think it would feel so satisfying to make something by hand. Even something as inelegant as this." Alexa looked around her.

"Thanks for building this with me, Alexa. It might be my tree, but the treehouse is as much yours as mine." He indicated around them. "You can use it anytime you like."

She gave him a high five. "My mom is wondering where I am. I have to go." She got up, threw her hoodie over her head and climbed down.

While her head was still inside the treehouse, she gave it one last perusal before nodding, "I like it."

The doorbell rang unexpectedly, and Ruth wondered who it could be. She checked the security feed of the camera by the door on her phone and saw a man in a gray coat standing there looking relaxed as he glanced up to the camera. Alexa wasn't there. She'd gone over to the treehouse for the second Saturday in a row.

Ruth opened the door.

"Can I help you?"

The man smiled at her, his gray eyes reminding her of James' eyes. He was as tall as well, but his hair was short and black whereas James' was blond. The man had a faint dark stubble on his face and faint wrinkles around his eyes, probably a few years older than her.

"Good morning, Ma'am. I'm from the Queen's community board. We like to interview new residents and make sure they settle into the area happily. If you have a few moments to spare, I won't take up much of your time." He gave her a disarming smile and she felt herself relax.

"I guess I have a few moments, Mister?"

"Where're my manners. I'm Isaac Smith."

"Well, Mr. Smith."

"Please, call me Isaac and you must be Mrs. Ruth Johnson according to my records."

"Yes. Please come in."

She turned around and he followed her in. The front door led into the lounge. She indicated that he should take a seat on the two-seater couch and sat down opposite him on the couch chair. He observed the bland brown fabric and the lack of decorations.

"You haven't unpacked everything yet, I see."

She blushed. "We are a bit minimalistic I'm afraid."

He nodded. "Nothing wrong with that. Give me a tidy

house any day."

She rubbed one hand over the top of the other. "What do you want to ask me?"

He pulled the leather satchel that hung over his shoulder forwards and took an iPad out of it. "Just a short survey. Let's start with question one: Why did you move to Queens?" He sat back; his pose relaxed.

Ruth broke eye contact and looked away, "Not any particular reason. We needed to be in New York, and this looked like the most affordable area to rent in."

"Why did you need to be in New York?" He slipped in casually as if he was just making conversation.

Ruth eyed him, her hands clasped together, "I'd prefer to keep that private."

"No worries." He looked down at his iPad "Have you felt welcomed by the community?"

She shrugged, "Everyone seems nice."

"Would you consider joining any community projects? I can give you a list. We have some interesting schemes where you can contribute and meet new people."

"Sure." Ruth looked past him towards the kitchen and the back door.

He cleared his throat, "How many people in your household?"

"Two." She settled her eyes on him again. He kept quiet so she expanded, "Me and my daughter."

"How old is she?"

"I don't see how that is relevant, Mr Smith."

He held his hand up, "Just want to help you settle in. We

have a few youth groups that she might enjoy.”

“How do you know she’s a teenager?” Ruth sat forward. “Where did you say you work again?”

The man’s body tensed. “For the Queens Community board, but I volunteer. My real work is in the city.”

She stared at him and he looked at his iPad. “Last question. Do you think that you will stay in Queens permanently or is it not the type of area you would consider long-term?”

A frown etched on her forehead, “I don’t think so.”

He nodded and gave her a smile. “Thank you for your time, Ruth.” He stood up. “May I use your bathroom?”

She walked him to the bathroom down the hallway, before going to the kitchen to fetch a drink. The man seemed innocent enough. Had she become paranoid after all these years?

She heard the toilet flush and after a few seconds he reappeared on the other side of the counter.

“Thank you again.”

Ruth released a heavy sigh, “I’m sorry if I seemed rude, Isaac. I’m not great with strangers. Can I offer you a drink?”

He turned back, his eyebrows lifted, “I get it. New in town, strange man on your doorstep wanting to know things about you. I’m harmless if that helps.” He grinned at her and she smiled back.

“I have orange juice and milk.” She blushed, “I mean tea or coffee, too.”

He sat down at the counter, looking at home, “I’ll take coffee if you’ll drink with me.”

She made the brew, aware of him quietly watching her. The coffee's aroma whiffed into the air.

"Thank you." He took it from her, and she slipped onto the seat next to him with hers.

He glanced at the ring on her finger and said, "I hope you'll be happy here in Queens. I've lived here all my life and it isn't as bad as the critics say."

"The reviews online said the same. I'm not sorry we moved here." She shifted her weight, took a sip and asked, "So what do you do in the city when you aren't out helping strangers settle into Queens?"

He grimaced, "Boring, I'm afraid. I'm an analyst."

"Analysing what?"

"My field is specifically analysing data on the impact we have on the environment through noise and sound."

Ruth's eyes widened, "That's not boring."

"It can be when you have to work through piles of data from all over the world."

"Do you monitor the noise impact?"

"We do. There is new data coming in all the time. Your turn. What do you do for a living?" He pinned her with a look that left her with no option but to answer.

"I'm a biotechnician." The moment she said it she glanced down at her coffee and bit her lower lip.

"Wow, that's an interesting field itself. I'm fascinated by the advances they've made in technology and DNA lately. Do you have a field of expertise?" He invited her to expand.

"No." She drained her cup and looked at her watch. "I'm sorry, I forgot that I have something I still need to do this morning. If you leave me the list of community groups, I'll see if I can join one." Getting up, she moved to the other side of the counter.

Isaac placed his cup down on the counter. "Thank you for that and your time. If you give me your number or email address, I'll send you the info."

She rattled off her email which he recorded on his iPad. He stood up and carried his mug to the sink before heading to the door. Ruth trailed behind him. On the step outside he gave her a two-fingered salute before walking down the sidewalk. She followed him with her eyes, pursing her lips.

Stop being paranoid, she reprimanded herself. At least Alexa hadn't come home during his visit. Wouldn't it be nice if he really were just a friendly member of the Queens community board and she was just a new person in the area? She shook her head. Normality was a thing she could only dream of.

They lay on the double bed watching the reflection of the lampshade twirl and swirl against the walls. The last Saturday of the month was their sleepover night. They watched a chick flick, ate chocolate and popcorn and just generally tried to have fun. Ruth had been looking forward to time with Alexa as she had been spending a lot of time with Oscar in the treehouse during the past few weeks. The movie had long ago finished. Alexa was lying very still. Ruth moved her hand and covered Alexa's with it.

"Thanks for watching with me."

"I enjoy seeing you enjoy something."

Ruth's lips pressed tight together, she mumbled thanks.

"Mom, what would you do if you had no cause?" The

hollowness in Ruth's chest made it hard for her to form a reply.

"Why do you ask?"

"Just imagining a different scenario."

It was quiet for a while. Haltingly, Ruth said, "I guess I would've just been a normal researcher. Married with children."

"Would you have liked more children?" Alexa pinned her with a stare.

"I don't know, but I do know I have the best daughter in the world." Ruth touched Alexa's cheek, and she turned into it, kissing her palm.

"Literally." That set them off giggling. After they grew quiet again, Alexa whispered, "I love you, Mom."

Ruth squeezed her eyes shut, trying to ward off the intense ache in her heart. "I love you too, Lexi."

Long after her mother's breathing had evened out, Alexa lay still on her side looking at her. At first, she had pretended to sleep, until she was sure Ruth had moved into a deeper sleep cycle. Staring at her now she memorized every laugh line, every inch of her face. She had to do this. For herself as much as for her parents.

Stealthily she crept out of the room into her own, where a small tote bag was hidden with essential things. For a minute she closed her eyes and focused on the spy camera she knew was in the living room. No one watching would notice there would be a missing minute in their recording. It was all it took for her to leave the house. There was an all-night bus terminal that went to the airport in the main road. Alexa threw her white hoodie over her head walking there at a clipped pace. There she bought a ticket in cash.

The timing was worked out so that she didn't loiter more than a minute in the bus terminal. In the back of the almost empty bus, she sank down low, out of sight of the onboard camera. That was almost too easy.

There was no going back now.

Sean rubbed his brow as if to ward off a headache. Every attempt they'd made to hack into the security cameras Ruth had around the house was thwarted in some way. It was a normal system which they'd easily hacked into at other places, but it wouldn't work. Almost as if someone else was countering their hacking. The listening device he'd left under the couch and by the kitchen sink wasn't responding either.

He flicked through the files he'd gathered on the couple and their associates. Along with all the information he had on their daughter. They had a very low online footprint. Before JJ's incarceration, they'd moved around a lot. He'd held down jobs at various high-profile companies like Apple, Microsoft and Intel. He even did a stint at AMG. JJ wasn't just an amazing programmer; he was an extremely good mechanical engineer as well.

He pulled Ruth's file up. There was very little on her. After completing her degree, she married JJ and had Alexa not long afterwards. There was no work information. To all appearances she chose to be a stay-at-home mother.

They lived a modest middle-class life. No grand holidays or expensive possessions. Apart from moving around for JJ's work, there was nothing to show. They didn't seem to have connections to the people from their past. Although he did trace a few students who studied with them to the New

York area. No connection to their families. Lone wolves.

He sat back in his seat, the tip of his pen between his teeth, "What are you up to?"

Getting up, he grabbed his jacket from off the hook. "I'm going out of town for a little."

Mole didn't look up. "See you when you get back."

There was an old professor of theirs that sparked Sean's interest. Perhaps an interview was in order.

CHAPTER 2

Professor Adam Anderson heard a noise at the door to his lab and looked up with a frown. He had been studying something through his electron microscope which fascinated him and hadn't wanted any interruptions.

"Langdon, is that you?"

He nudged his glasses back on his nose, through which his green eyes seemed magnified. The boy's mother would've had a fit if she saw how he brought up their son which included working on Sundays. Sundays used to be their family day. For a short time they were a family, anyway.

Unexpected remorse stirred in him but when his fifteen-year-old son pushed open the door, his blond curls almost as unruly as his father's brown ones, he couldn't help but smile.

When his wife died, he hired a nanny for his one-year-old son. As Langdon grew older, he chose to home-school him. Basically, taking him along to all his conferences across the globe and encouraging him to learn whatever he was

interested in. He blinked a few times.

Langdon grinned at him, with a mischievous sparkle in his green eyes, "If you stare at me any longer, I might alter the form and show my true nature."

The professor gave a slight start and shook his head. "Sorry."

Langdon plonked his skateboard down by the couch in the corner and sauntered over to the table. He glanced at the invisible specimen under the microscope.

"What are you looking at?"

His father shook his head and looked down without comprehension. "I-I'm not sure. Langdon, are you happy?"

A deep sigh escaped Langdon's tall frame, "What's up with you, Dad? You've been giving me that weird stare a lot lately and asked me this about three times in the past few months."

He walked around the table and placed his hand on his dad's shoulder. They were the same height, so they could look eye to eye.

"I'm happy, Dad. I wouldn't exchange this life for any other. I don't miss friends or school. I've got friends all over the globe and hundreds online. If I had to prove my education through some silly test, I would probably score above the highest percentile. You've done good. Mom would've been proud."

His dad's face relaxed into a smile and he pulled Langdon into a hug. "I love you, son. You're my..."

"Best invention..." Langdon laughingly said as he pulled back. "I know, you must have told me a million, zillion times. If I didn't know any better, I'd start thinking I'm an android, and I don't know it."

His dad's smile faltered, as another memory from long ago surfaced. A memory he wanted to forget.

They both looked up as the metal door opened with a silent whoosh and an unexpected visitor entered their sanctuary. It was a girl, with shoulder-length blonde hair and blue eyes. Langdon's eyes widened; she was beautiful.

"Professor Adam Anderson?" Her soft, modulated voice startled them. It had no accent. Eerily it sounded almost like the virtual assistant found online.

"That's me." The professor cleared his throat. "Can I help you?"

"I hope so. Do you remember the project you were involved with fourteen years ago? Project Salem."

The Prof. visibly paled. Langdon looked from the girl to

his father, "What's going on, Dad?"

"My name is Alexa and I'm the product of that project." The professor gasped. Holding onto the table with white-knuckled hands.

Langdon frowned, "Listen, you're scaring my dad. I don't care what he's done before, he's a decent man. I think you need to leave."

Instead she stepped nearer to them, "I'm sorry. I didn't intend to scare him. I need his help." This time she looked straight into Langdon's eyes and he was momentarily distracted by their vivid blue.

"You can't be. They didn't really do it, did they?" The professor's voice was laced with disbelief, mixed with something like awe.

She smiled at him. "They did. Do you remember Ruth Clarke and James Johnson? I'm their actual daughter."

The professor shook his head. "I can't believe it."

She inclined her head and before their astonished eyes, her clothes reshaped from the tracksuit and T-shirt she was wearing into jeans and a flowered top. Her hair also adjusted into the same brown shade as the professor's.

The profs' eyes were popping out of his head, "You, you can control them? Send them where you want to and reprogram them to do anything you like? Bu-but we never thought that would be possible. How is that possible?"

She stared down at her hands, "After they established the interface in my brain, they found that I started interfacing with the nanobots as well. Basically, if I imagine what I want to do, it programs them to do it."

Quietly the professor asked, "How many do you have?"

She shrugged as if it didn't matter, "Trillions. I don't have time to explain now. I'm being tracked and I need you to dispose of the inbuilt chip they've placed in me."

The man went rigid, "What do you mean tracked? Are you running away?"

"Professor, you have an idea of what they want to use me for. I'm sure you would agree that fleeing is the best option." Her face was expressionless, her eyes serious as they engaged with the professors.

He swallowed visibly, before inquiring, "Where is the tracker?"

Langdon moved out of the way, his head abuzz with what he was hearing and seeing. His dad looked at him as if he had forgotten that he was there.

"Langdon, won't you go fetch us some lunch from the takeout place across the street?"

Langdon frowned; it wasn't like his dad to be thinking about food at a time like this. He clearly wanted him out of the way.

The girl fixed her blue stare on Langdon, "Don't worry. I won't be here long, but you might need to go into hiding for a little while."

With a last reluctant look at his dad who gave him a tremulous smile, he left, hurrying along the long hallway. Their familiar building felt sinister, as if unknown enemies were lurking in it.

Alexa frowned. "I'm sorry."

The professor looked up, "You'll take care of him if something happens to me, please? I was always afraid of this. That my sins would catch up with me."

She remained quiet before saying, "You didn't mean for it to be used this way, professor. Idealism has a way of overtaking rational thinking. The tracker is behind between my shoulder blades. If you feel around, you should feel the disk, embedded under my skin."

He located it, marvelling at her shirt which opened before him like a small portal. "You need a surgeon, not a professor."

"You were the only one I could trust, and you know how to work with delicate things. I heal quickly and I can supress the pain sensors. So please proceed."

After locating a small, very sharp knife, and taking numerous deep breaths, he brought the edge close to her skin. "Are you sure about this?"

"Yes."

She stood perfectly still as he cut through her skin, it didn't bleed very much, as if she had directed the blood away. The chip was easy to find and he pulled it out, holding it with a tweezers, while her skin started healing before his eyes.

"Could I?"

"Yes."

He grabbed a small portable electronic microscope and focused on where she was healing. Immediately it looked like a scene out of a space movie. Thousands of little nanobots were scurrying to and fro, activating the rebuilding and generating cells.

A tear ran down his cheek. "It actually works."

She turned around and placed her hand on his shoulder. "You did well. Maybe one day, it will save people's lives."

Her body stiffened, and she looked up, "They are here.

You need to hide!"

A sudden determination seemed to have seized the professor, "No, there is a back exit, through the side lab, behind the cupboard in the corner. I'll stall them. Take Langdon with you, please."

She dipped her head and ran into the next room. The cupboard in the corner was easy for her to move, and she slipped through the exit unseen, just as she heard the other door open.

Carefully she shut the opening behind her, went around the corner and ran across the road to the takeout store where Langdon could be seen clutching two cokes on a tray and a brown paper bag in the other. He saw her dart across the road and stop three meters from him as a shudder went through her. He glimpsed sorrow on her face for a split second before she reached him.

"I'm sorry. We have to run and hide."

"What about my dad?"

She looked at him, her eyes brimming with tears; it simultaneously terrified and comforted him.

"I'm sorry, Langdon, they were nearer than I thought. He wanted me to escape and take care of you." She looked across the road. "We need to hide. Now."

"I know a place," Langdon responded instinctively. Adrenaline set in when he sighted the men in black coming out of the building opposite. He handed her the coke, linked his arm through hers and led her around the corner out of their sight.

They crossed a few more streets before he went down three stairs that led to a door with no number or handle on the side of a building. Knocking in what sounded like Morse code resulted in the door opening from the inside and they hurried down into a dark room illuminated only by a dozen computer screens.

A scrawny young man gave them a grin. "Wow, Lang, hot date. Is that burgers I smell?" He grabbed the packet from Langdon, and took one of the burgers out, flopping back into an old office chair which he wheeled back, and swivelled around to face his monitors.

Langdon sank down in the only other chair opposite.

"Have some coke." Alexa offered the takeaway cup to him. He took it and drank, finding the sweet liquid helping with the weakness that had seized him.

"You going to introduce us or what?" The question came from the guy between bites of the burger, as he still stared at his screens.

"This is Pip. Pip, this is Alexa." Langdon introduced them on auto-pilot.

"What can I do for you?" Came the sudden voice of the virtual assistant.

Pip swivelled around with a grin, "Nice one. Nothing thanks, Alexa."

Alexa grinned back at him, "Lexi will do."

"Nice to meet you Lexi. Why has Lang here brought you to my lair?"

"We need your help."

Langdon looked at her numbly. His thoughts felt disjointed with the knowledge that they had left his father back there, possibly dead.

"I'll do anything I can for my buddy Lang here." Pip finished off his burger and wiped his mouth on his sleeve.

"So, what will it be?"

"May I use your computer?"

Pip's eyebrows rose, "You want to touch my baby?" After a moment, he shrugged, "Sure, why not? I guess you couldn't do that much harm."

He stood up and offered her his seat with a little bow. "All yours."

"Thank you." She sat down and unexpectedly the screens started moving and changing, flicking through different sites faster than they could see what was on them.

Pip took a few steps back, and crouched next to Langdon, in a whisper he said, "Am I seeing what I'm seeing? Or are you playing one of your practical jokes?"

Langdon hadn't been giving the monitors any attention, battling the urging he had to go back to the lab. Now, he looked across and his eyes widened. The stillness was eerie.

"I can interact with the electromagnetic signals." She spoke without looking at them.

Pip went over to her and looked between her and the screens, waving his hand a few times between Alexa and the screens.

"I don't believe this. Are you from the future or something?" For the first time, he looked at Langdon with a worried crease on his forehead, "Is this one of your father's inventions?"

A screen popped up, which showed the inside of Professor Adam Anderson's lab. Langdon gave a startled cry as he sprang up and looked over her shoulder. There was no sign of his father.

Alexa was frowning. "I heard a gunshot, but there isn't

any blood on the floor and no body. Maybe they only scared him and took him as a hostage."

"Whoa, whoa, whoa! Who are *they*?" Pip's voice had gone up an octave as he wrung his hands together.

"The guys hunting Alexa."

"How can I help you?"

"I mean Lexi." Langdon pulled his hand through his hair, his heart felt like it was in a vice grip. He struggled to breathe.

The screens had been moving again and Alexa spoke, "I've checked the footage, and they had a van at the back. The feed stops after they enter the building, so we cannot see if they took him with them, but it is probable they did.

"How do we find him?" Langdon forced out; his fists clenched by his sides.

Alexa turned to him, "I've erased you from the system. You have a new identity as an eighteen-year-old student called Langdon White, complete with a background story as well as a bank account with enough money in to see you through for a while. You need to rent a new apartment under your new name and stay low, off the radar.

Pip whistled through his teeth, "You did all that now?"

"But I need to find my dad." Langdon clenched his jaw. "You can't stop me."

She got up and stood in front of him. "I'm not trying to stop you. He asked me to take care of you. I've done that now. If anyone looks for you, you died seven years ago. Except for physical photos, there are no other photos of you." She looked at Pip, "I've upgraded your system. It is now more secure. I can't tell you who is hunting me without placing you in danger."

"My father is in danger because of you!" Langdon's voice shook. "How am I supposed to find him, if I don't even know where to start?"

"I don't know why they took him. He can't be of any use to them."

"What if they told you to turn yourself in or they'll kill him?"

She seemed to mull it over, "If you had to choose between saving your father or saving millions of people, which would it be?"

Langdon stared into her mesmerizing blue eyes, "That's not fair."

She looked down, "No, it isn't." Her shoulders slumped.

As she started for the door, Langdon grabbed her arm, "Lexi, where are you going?"

She stood still, "I do not know. As far away from civilization as possible. Maybe Iceland or the Amazon. I need to disappear. The world isn't ready for my technology yet."

"Did my dad help create you?"

"Indirectly. He designed the original nanobots."

"Is she a robot?" Pip's jaw was literally hanging on the floor. "Like, a real, living Alexa?" "How can I help you?"

All three of them burst out in laughter, which broke the tension of the moment. "No, Pip, I'm human, but advanced through technology. Thank you for allowing me to use your baby. Look after yourselves." With that, she stepped out the door and they were left together in the room.

A processor fan started up, shattering the stillness while Langdon sat down where Alexa had sat. On the main screen was the address of an estate agency in a suburban part of town, far away from the lab. Another screen had a bank address on. All in all, between all the screens there was everything he needed to start a new life. The printer started to live and printed off a birth certificate.

Pip picked it up, "Well, Langdon White, welcome to New York City." He scratched his head, "I don't know about you, but wouldn't your dad want you to help this girl too? Maybe if you helped her, you could find your dad."

"Help her? You have *no* idea what she is capable of. I don't think she needs anyone's help."

"So, you're just going to let one of your father's greatest inventions, which by the way, he was willing to save with his life, go rust away in the North Pole or the Amazon?"

Langdon shook his head, "Pip, have I told you lately that you are a genius."

Pip smirked. "Not lately no, but I know. I'm going to start digging up everything I can find about nanobots." He rubbed his hands together.

"She mentioned two people, Ruth Clarke and James Johnson,"

"Not *the* James Johnson?"

"What do you mean?"

"Dude, don't you remember? A few months ago, they arrested only the greatest hacker ever, James Johnson or JJ as they called him on the web."

Langdon frowned and then his face lit up, "I remember! Isn't he the guy who hacked every major government and intelligence agency and released their dirty secrets all over the web?

"That's the one."

"It makes no sense. I'm sure she said he was her father."

"What?"

"It sounded like my father knew them, and that he worked with them on a project called, uh, I can't remember."

Pip hit him on the back, "It'll come back to you, but how are you going to find this Lexi girl?"

Langdon rubbed his chin, "I have an idea."

He went outside, stood in the deserted alley and said aloud, "Alexa, I don't think my dad would save your life just so that you can go and rot away somewhere. There must be a way we can stop these people. I've got some skills and connections too and I'd like to help you."

He waited, and before long she appeared at the top of the alley. Her hair was back to being blond and she sported a white hoodie, covering most of it.

She walked up to him, "Are you sure?"

"Yes."

"Thank you."

They stared at each other for another moment.

"Friends?" He said, holding out his hand.

She inclined her head with a small smile, "Friends."

Sean cursed under his breath. Just his luck to arrive at the professor's lab in time to see armed guys hefting the unconscious professor out the back and into their van. He'd walked round to the back to scout out the place before going in and had had to make himself scarce before the men noticed him. Crossing the street to the safety of the takeout place, he bought himself a milkshake. Seating himself on the high red stool by the window, he observed two of the men dressed in black scouting the street up and down. Who were they looking for?

Experience had taught him that the patient man usually got his prey. There was no point in trying to follow them to try and help the professor. Better to wait and see if the person they obviously didn't get might come back to the lab. He decided to stake out the place for the next twenty-four hours and in the night, he'd search the place from top to bottom. Sending a message to Mole, he asked him to freeze the video feeds of the lab's security system between one and two in the morning. There must be a very good reason the professor got taken. And his instinct was telling him it had something to do with the girl in Queens.

Ruth reached for her phone in the kitchen, just to set it down again. The special code she could text was ingrained in her brain. 101333. She never thought she would need to use it. It signaled the failure of the past few months or rather the past fourteen years of their lives. She wiped her hand across her face, her tired, red-rimmed eyes glancing at the clock. One o'clock in the morning. How long had it been since she found the note on her bedside table?

Such a simple little note, but it felt like an explosive bomb in her hand. She failed. The one thing she was supposed to do, and she failed. James' face when she'd tell him played in her mind's eye and she shuddered and clutched her stomach with her arms.

Maybe she should run away too. She thought of Lexi, her own flesh and blood daughter running away and for a second the anguish she had kept under wraps during all fourteen years of their experiment surfaced. Ruth's body crumpled in on itself, rocking back and forth, while her uncontrollable sobs echoed through the empty house.

A memory came to her. The first time she held her tiny little baby girl in her arms. Her soft little body was so perfect, so beautiful. Then the biotechnicians whisked her away, tearing out a part of Ruth's heart with it. She sacrificed her own baby, for the good of all mankind. It should have made her feel proud, but in that moment, she felt like she had done a horrible thing.

And so, it continued every time they started with a new round of injections and she held her daughter's hand, soothing her, explaining why they needed to do this, all the while thinking how hollow it sounded in her own ears. And now, her daughter confirmed her innermost feelings with her own refusal to comply. She pressed her fist to her mouth, getting up. Dizziness made her pause for a moment.

Ruth trailed to Lexi's room for the hundredth time that day. She sat down on the bed and stared up at the shelf full of teddy bears. She got her one for every birthday. She hadn't taken even one with her. The bookshelf didn't have any books on it. They had to travel light, and digital books were faster and easier to access. It dawned on her that her daughter had taken nothing with her at all. She didn't need anything. She didn't need them. Lungs constricting, she fought for a breath.

Another memory surfaced. They were all gathered in Professor Li Geming's private rooms where he gave extra-curricular classes to a few select. At first, she couldn't believe that he'd chosen her. Her grades were good, but she wasn't one of the popular students at campus. Besides her handful of friends, she had mostly kept to herself.

They'd been meeting for a few months with the professor progressively leading them into debates about the different ways they could have a positive impact on the world. During this session something happened. They were all there. Eight students. Four men and four women.

The professor stared them down with his dark narrow eyes. "Can you imagine a world governed by an unbiased Artificial Intelligence? Do you think that would bring the order we need?"

They sat mulling it over. James spoke first, "We haven't even developed a real Artificial Intelligence. The ones in the movies don't count." Everybody chuckled.

"What is the problem? Why haven't we achieved this?"

Evan said, "It can't learn like a human. It can't interact with the world enough." Christine smiled at him. Those two were clearly in love.

Ruth said, "What if we could create a way for an AI to connect with a human and learn as the human grows?" She looked at the professor and saw his eyes gleam. Obviously, he'd thought of the same thing but was delighted that she hit upon the right idea.

Beatrice piped up, "We were learning about nanobots in class today. But it's only a theory, so far we haven't successfully made any."

Stanley added, "So you're thinking in theory if we had nanobots we could send them into someone's brain and program them to interact with an Artificial Intelligence."

"That's genius!" James clapped his hands. Ruth wished she'd said that.

"I know someone who is on the brink of developing nanobots that will actually work." Professor Li dropped that bomb into their midst quietly as if he were sharing a state secret.

The group buzzed with excitement.

The professor indicated that he wanted to say something. "You realise that a breakthrough in technology like this will be snapped up by the world. But if we can keep it under wraps and use it to develop an advanced Artificial Intelligence who can bring a new world order, it could transform everyone's lives for the better. We can bring the age of Salem. Peace."

The students stared at their professor with wide eyes. Their hearts were racing. They were being asked to be part of something big, something that could reshape the world.

"I'm in," James said without hesitation. One by one they

assented. Ruth was last.

She blinked furiously, wiping at her cheeks. That was the worst decision of her life; perhaps her greatest flaw, was blindly following without really thinking for herself. Wanting to fit in and not go against the flow.

The other fateful choice came two years later, the day the professor called her and James into his office alone.

"Please shut the door, James." He requested as he motioned them to take a seat across from them.

"I've evaluated everyone in the group. You and Ruth show the greatest potential to be the couple who generates the child and brings it up."

They sat in shocked silence. James cleared his throat. "We aren't a couple, Sir."

"That is exactly why I've chosen you. It will be easier to conduct this as an experiment if there are fewer feelings involved. It won't be your child but would belong to the Salem group. It will be our project."

Ruth swallowed. She felt partly relieved that nobody had noticed her infatuation with the handsome James. But whether she could hide it forever, being in such close contact with him she didn't know. Her heart was beating wildly in her chest. This was her one chance to make a difference in the world.

She wasn't throwing it away. "I'll do it." She spoke startling the two men.

James pinned her with his gray eyes, "Are you sure? It will mean you can't marry anyone else. I don't mind. What I mean is, I haven't planned on marrying anyway so it will suit me." He looked away.

"I don't mind either. I want to help create a fairer world." Ruth sounded more confident than she felt.

"It's settled then. I'll have your marriage arranged before a judge for next week to keep up appearances and then we can start to procreate within three months. You're dismissed."

A cold shiver ran down Ruth's back as she thought back to that day. Everything about it was wrong, but she was too blind to see it. All she felt was elation that she got to be with James even though he didn't want her. She crawled in under the blankets wishing it smelled of her daughter, but there was nothing. The room felt as empty as she felt inside. She had no choice. She lifted the phone, still clutched in her hand and punched in the code. Maybe he'd understand.

Ten seconds later her phone rang.

"What happened?" James sounded wide awake.

"Lexi ran away." She sounded as washed out as she felt.

"When?" He quietly questioned.

"Sometime last night. I found a note this morning next to the bed."

"And you waited until now to alert me?" His voice was still quiet, but with the tone, he might as well have shouted.

"I hoped she would change her mind and come back." Ruth pulled herself into a smaller ball.

"What does the note say?" She recited it to him, by now she knew it off by heart.

"Did you know she was feeling this way?"

"No!" Ruth shook her head, cringing inside. She couldn't tell him about their conversations. Looking back, she knew she should've seen the signs, but at the time she thought she'd convinced her.

"Some mother you make." His cold words washed over her like acid. "Everything we've worked for, sacrificed for, and you let it walk out the door?"

Something in Ruth snapped, "You seem to forget she's not just a project, she's our daughter too! Did you want *her* locked up?"

Silence met her and the phone signalled that it disconnected. Ruth started trembling. It was out of her hands now. She knew James would contact the others. In fact, she had been tracking Alexa through the day, realizing that she was making her way towards their old friend and colleague, Professor Anderson in Berkeley.

She'd lied to James, almost willing Alexa to escape. The tracker hadn't left the professor's lab since lunch time, making her wonder why. Maybe he removed it for her, but why didn't he destroy it? Her head was pounding. She fell into a fitful sleep in her daughter's bed, clutching one of the teddy bears.

The knock at the door disturbed the man sitting at the massive ornate desk in an office the size of the president of the United States' office.

"Come in." He barked.

A man came in, dressed in a black suit. "She got away, Sir. They have the professor in custody." His tone betrayed nothing.

The other man frowned, his dark, tanned skin and perfect complexion belying the fact that he was in his fifties. As he stood up, he moved with the agility of a young man.

Even his black hair showed no signs of gray. Despite his attractiveness, there was no wedding ring on his finger. He came to a standstill in front of his desk.

"How did she get away?"

The man shifted his eyes away from the penetrating brown ones of his employer. "The professor removed her tracker before we got there, Sir."

The silence in the room hung heavy.

"Dismissed." The short command caused the man to turn and hasten from the room. The other man watched him with narrowed eyes wishing he could vent his fury on him, but it wasn't the way to get good help. He flexed his hands, releasing a breath.

The man didn't know what they were up against anyhow. This thought made him grimace. At least he had an advantage over her. Her misguided love for humanity would be her downfall.

He strode over to the window and leaned on the sill, staring out across the immaculate gardens. He had another secret weapon she knew nothing about, and he was going to use it to capture her, replace her and achieve his dream. Straightening, he held his hands loosely behind his back. Salem would happen no matter what. His dark brows furrowed together.

First, he needed to get rid of everyone who knew about the project. He turned to his desk, picked up his phone and dialled a number.

"Execute Plan B." He rang off and sat back drumming his fingers against his leg. It was only a slight bump in the road, a small delay. He was going to sacrifice a lot more for the cause in order to achieve his goal. It would be worth it in the end though.

James lay still, letting the disappointment wash over him as the heaviness spread through his limbs. They were so close. It was only days till Alexa was supposed to put into motion the event that would lead him to be invited into the inner sanctuary of the NIRT; The National Incident Response Team.

All their plans seemed to tumble down like a house of cards and he clenched his jaw together. He'd been in this prison for three months. If they found her, they could change her mind. He could simply be captured again and still execute the plan, but he knew they would never do that without him, he would have to break out.

Ruth's face appeared as he remembered it. He rubbed his hand across his face. There was no time for foolish emotions in all of this. After they established Salem there would be plenty of time to worry about relationships. Time for his Plan B.

The next morning during breakfast he used the pre-arranged sign to signal the guard they had on their payroll. He gave one nod towards James and left the room. A few minutes later, James left too. The guard had a key to a storage room down the hall, which they locked themselves into. James and the guard exchanged clothes. Hidden in the room were make-up and false hair, beards and contact lenses.

It took a matter of minutes to transform James into someone resembling the guard, with dark eyes instead of gray. Dark hair instead of blond. The guard was called Gary and James made it look like he had tied him up on the storage cupboard's floor. He locked the door behind him and sauntered back to the breakfast room. Gary's shift was ending just after breakfast, thankfully before roll call.

James walked out of the prison, scanning his personnel card. The biometric scanner for his eyes proved no problem. The lenses he had in weren't ordinary lenses. They had been pre-made to reflect the same eye pattern as Gary's. James clicked the black SUV's remote and heard it beep towards the back of the parking lot. He got in and drove off.

A few blocks away, he parked it before sprinting off. Less than a mile from there he opened a storage door that had another car stashed inside. He pulled the dust sheet off the blue corvette with relish and started her up. In her trunk was everything he needed to disappear.

He changed into a new outfit that was stashed in the car. His favourite black jeans Levi's and a blue Levi T-shirt. A bit dusty, but he hadn't felt this comfortable in a long time. Adding a baseball cap and dark glasses, his disguise was complete. With the satnav set to Ruth and Alexa's address, he cruised along the highway with the radio pumping music into the air. He was home free. By the time they discovered Gary, he would be long gone.

He found the address in Queens easily, coasting past the house a few times to make sure he hadn't been tailed before turning in. The garage was unlocked, and he stowed away his car with relief. Before he opened the internal door, he took a deep breath gearing up to face Ruth. He climbed the three steps, opened the door and instantly realised the house was empty. It had that silent feel of a house abandoned.

A quick search confirmed it. There were no personal

effects anywhere except for a laptop on the kitchen countertop.

There was a note on top of it. 'I think everything is bugged.' James frowned. He had a special security firm check every place they went to and personally checked all their gear. For all her faults, Ruth wasn't prone to paranoia. She was very smart; sometimes he wondered if she was smarter than him.

He shook his head and pretended to take the laptop under his arm and leave the house, but instead, he stayed in the corner by the door and studied the living room looking for anything out of the ordinary. He looked up at the ceiling and his gaze travelled over the fire alarm only to come back to it. There was something different about this one. It seemed like it was only a different brand, but he instinctively knew it was a state-of-the-art listening and recording device. Why didn't the company pick it up? Then it hit him. They must have installed it.

A sense of urgency rose in him, and he placed the laptop down on the floor, hurrying to the trunk of the car. Taking a black tote bag out, he gently let the trunk lid down. After retrieving the laptop, he made his way to the side door in the garage that led to the back garden. Once outside, he ran over the grass and scrambled over the fence which conveniently had a ladder leaning against it.

"Hey Mister!"

Startled, James looked around for the source of the voice and found a bush of snow-white frizzy hair framing a translucent white face in the tree house above him.

"Are you Alexa's dad?"

James dipped his chin.

"Come up here. She gave me something to give to you."

Carefully James looked around the area, giving a peek over the fence to make sure there was no one watching before he clambered up the sturdy, wooden ladder. Inside was simply a square floor with walls, but there were two comfortable blue bean bags and a small plastic table with biscuits and juice on. James sank down on one of the bean bags, placing his tote bag next to him and the laptop on his lap.

"My name is Oscar. I'm Alexa's friend. We built this treehouse together."

James' eyes widened and he looked at the treehouse with new eyes before settling them on Oscar again, "Hi, Oscar, I'm James. Do you know where she is?"

Oscar gave a little shake of his head. "But she did give me this for you." He produced a sealed white, rectangular envelope and handed it to James. There was only one word on the front: *Dad*. James stared at it, for some reason feeling a thickness in his throat.

"She loves you; you know."

He looked at the strange boy across him. "What did you say?"

"I said, she loves you. She told me so much about you. She thinks you are amazing."

James blinked, "What exactly did she tell you?"

Oscar shrugged, "Oh lots of things, like how you taught her to ride her first bike and took her camping in the mountains and read her stories at bedtime."

The protest on James' lips fell away when he realised that Alexa had told Oscar all the normal things a dad would've done with their daughter. In fact, he had done none of that. He searched his memory for anything normal that he had done with her and came up empty. Just like his own parents. His reproachful words towards Ruth sounded in his head. She wasn't a lousy mother; he was a lousy father.

"Are you all right?" Oscar's soft question hung in the air.

James stared at him and down at the envelope in his hand.

"I have to go."

The next moment the treehouse shook as the noise of an explosion vibrated through the air. James crawled over to the window facing towards the house where Ruth and Alexa had lived and found dust and rubble instead. It must have been rigged the whole time. Fear clutched in his gut. They were being targeted, but by whom? Maybe they had Alexa already and they just wanted to take out everyone who knew about her? Ruth!

Oscar tugged at his hand and he looked at him. "Someone blew up your house!"

"No sweat."

"Do you need a getaway car?"

James felt himself grin despite the seriousness of the situation. "Do you have one?"

"Follow me."

James followed the boy through his garden gate to the front of the street. A car parked across the road next to the curb gave a beep.

Oscar handed him a key. "Alexa said to give you this if something happened."

The car was a grey Cadillac CTS V. James scanned it with admiration. Alexa sure knew what type of ride he liked. Did she want him to find her? It didn't make sense. He rubbed his neck and glanced down at the boy.

"Thanks, Oscar."

"I'll be praying for you." The boy smiled up at him, his light blue eyes warm.

The "I don't need your prayers" sentence on his lips died a silent death. Instead, he nodded, quickly walked across the road, got into the car and drove off without a backward glance.

CHAPTER 3

James drove to East Rutherford as fast as the speed limit allowed. No sense in drawing unwanted attention to himself although he had a false identity card and driver's license on him. How compromised were they? He needed to contact Professor Li Geming.

First, he had to find Ruth. Protocol said she went into hiding with other team members in the group. Evan and Christine Palmer lived near their intended target as a second base for operations. They were both biotechnicians who helped program Alexa's nanobots. As before, he circled their block, knowing that their property could be compromised too. He itched to use his burner phone to ring Ruth, but her phone was probably bugged. He'd be alarmed if she still had it on her.

Deciding to park a few houses down, he left his bag in the car and strolled down the sidewalk, his cap pulled down low over his face. Counting down the numbers, he saw the right one. A glance into the window showed brightly-colored curtains, hippie style. He walked past

slowly, his hands in his pockets, trying to look like a man just out for a stroll. Crossing the road, he walked back again.

He'd almost reached his car before he heard footsteps behind him. Without looking back, he climbed in. Three seconds later the passenger door opened, and Ruth slid into the car with him. She had a small bag with her, which she placed by her feet. An awkward silence hovered between them. James racked his brain for something appropriate to say.

She sighed. "Was it bugged?"

"Yes. It also blew up."

Her eyes grew large. "What?"

"Did you warn them and the others?"

She nodded. "They'll find another place and go incognito. I left my new burner phone number with them."

"Text them to get out quickly. We don't know if their house is rigged too."

Ruth got the small phone out of her bag and sent the text. Her hands were shaking. He started up the car and they drove off.

"Where is Alexa?" James sounded angrier than he felt.

"She was last seen at the private lab of Professor Anderson." Ruth angled away from him.

"In Berkeley!" He mulled that over for a second before giving her a glance, "What do you mean last seen?"

Ruth clasped her hands together on her lap, not looking at him. "She arrived there around noon yesterday. Her tracker has stayed in the lab since then."

"You think he removed it for her?" James didn't wait for a reply. "We need to go to The Facility."

Ruth bit her lower lip, "Who do you think is after us?"

The lines on his forehead indented, "It could be anyone, CIA and FBI included. I don't understand it though. We've made sure we stay well under the radar."

"Could they have been watching us; connecting us to you?"

"I don't think so. I haven't been around you that much and we've moved locations separately every time. I was sure I'd covered our tracks." His jaw was clenched, his lips pressed together.

Ruth gave him a quick glance before looking away. "It's not your fault."

James brows pinched together.

"No matter. We need to find Alexa before anyone else does."

For the first time Ruth showed signs of fear, her voice tremulous, "What if they've got her, James?"

"What ifs won't get us anywhere. We need facts and The Facility will be the best place."

"Are you sure we aren't being tracked?"

He didn't answer. Twenty minutes later he pulled into the first fuel station he saw off the highway they were on. Parking round the back, in a corner furthest from other cars he methodically started looking through the car and both their bags. He inspected the phones and laptop they had with them in detail.

"Should I get us some coffee?"

"Here, use cash." He offered her a few notes from his wallet. "Take this too." He took off his cap and placed it on her head along with handing her his dark sunglasses.

"Thanks." She took in his shaved head; he could see she was stifling a grin. His face, neck and ears started feeling impossibly hot even though the air was chilly. She turned away but his eyes stayed on her as she made her way to the shop.

A memory surfaced.

"I'd like to introduce to you the newest member of our group. Miss Ruth Clarke." Professor Li Geming smiled at them. James took in the young woman standing next to the professor. Short, curvy with long auburn hair framing her face. Flawless white skin with a smattering of freckles across the bridge of her nose. She wore a pretty blue summer dress patterned with white daisies.

Their eyes connected and he smiled. Getting up, he gave a mock bow and indicated to the empty chair next to him. "Empty seat for a Queen next to the King." Everyone laughed at his joke, but she went beet red. She took the seat but kept herself turned away from him during the meeting. *Great going, James.* He pulled a face. From then on, he pretended he wasn't interested in her.

He dragged his hand through his hair and turned around exhaling loudly. *Focus, James. Fix the problem.* He took out his burner phone and punched in a number he knew well.

It rang without answer. His pulse increased as he tried again.

"Hello?"

"It's me."

"What happened?"

"She's run away, and we're being targeted."

"By whom?"

"I don't know."

"Find her!"

"I will."

"Don't go to The Facility."

"But—"

"—too risky. Set up a base and use your skills to track her down. She must have left a trail."

"Okay."

The phone went dead in his ear, and he looked at it, the lines in his forehead deeper than before. Getting out his laptop he searched for a hotel on the way to Berkeley, as well as a place to stay over in Berkeley the next day. He booked that one for a week under an alias he had in place for Ruth. Hopefully whoever was hunting them didn't know it.

Packing the laptop away, his hands started getting itchy to get on the move. *What was taking her so long?* He stared hard at the building while tapping his fingers on the roof of the car. After a few minutes, she appeared with two takeout coffees and a bag with more stuff. The smell of burger permeated his nostrils as she came nearer, and his impatience settled down. He was hungry. They got on the way, he starting in on the burger straight away. After he wolfed it down, he took a sip of the coffee.

"Thanks."

She was tucking into her own one. "Pleasure. When last did you eat?"

He shrugged, trying to remember if he had breakfast in prison that morning. It felt like days ago.

"Prison food sucks."

"I'm sure. It must have been hard."

"Not worse than boarding school."

She inclined her head. "You hated boarding school."

They drank their coffee in silence as the miles sped past under their wheels.

He found it strange that she didn't question where they were going. It was clear that they were heading away from The Facility by now.

Another memory stirred up from the past. Alexa was two years old. He walked into their bedroom and found Ruth on the floor beside the bed with a pile of tissues. Before he could turn around and leave, she saw him and that familiar embarrassed red flush flooded her face. She started gathering the tissues. He shifted his weight from one leg to the other.

"Something wrong?" He ventured.

She shook her head. "No. Nothing's wrong." She made it sound like a bad thing.

"Is that why you're crying?" He couldn't help himself.

A fresh sprinkle of tears started coming and he wanted to bolt. "Yes. She's so perfect. No booboos for me to kiss better. I can't comfort her. Mother her."

"Most moms would kill for a toddler like this."

"I know." The tears started falling faster and James left the room. It made no sense to him how a brilliant biotechnician like Ruth could have such irrational emotions. Give him wires and predictable code any day. A good thing they didn't marry for love. He would've sucked at being a real husband. The memory stung.

He exhaled and asked what he knew he had to.

"Are you worried about Alexa?"

Ruth shifted in her seat, rubbing her one hand over the other, "It feels silly. She is more capable than anyone but..."

"You still worry. I get it. You are a good mother, Ruth. Sorry about what I said earlier. I didn't mean it." He wanted to touch her hand but he didn't.

Tears pooled in her eyes, but she wiped them off quickly. Very quietly she ventured, "Do you ever regret—"

James steeled his face, "What use is it, Ruth? We made our choices long ago. There is no going back. I still believe in the cause, the new world we're going to create. It will be worth it in the end. I know it." *It had to be.*

She didn't reply but shifted to gaze out of the window.

Was Ruth doubting the cause? That would make her a liability. A weak link. She wouldn't betray them. She could never offer up Alexa. Or could she? His stomach felt knotted. He glanced over at her, tilting his head with narrowed eyes. *What if?*

Langdon briefly closed his eyes after the door shut behind them. It had been a hectic two days. Finally, he had a two-bedroom apartment in his name and a bank card and identity documents. Alexa had created an identity for herself as his younger sister, with him as her legal guardian. Thankfully, he was used to being in adult company and being independent. Nobody ever suspected he wasn't eighteen.

He ordered pizza to be delivered and sank down into the soft green couch, compliments of the fully furnished apartment. They had bought a laptop which Alexa was studying in that science fiction way of hers; springing through screens without touching the keyboard. He got up and walked over to the white kitchen island to peer over her shoulder.

"What are you looking for?"

"I'm trying to work out who the people were that took your father. At first, I thought it was our group, but my mother only contacted them after the men abducted your father."

"It could be anyone then. How will we ever find him?" He wiped across his face.

A picture popped up of a house that had imploded on itself. "Whose house was that?"

"Mine. They blew it up this afternoon, but my father got away."

"You mean, he's out of prison?" Langdon rubbed the back of his neck.

"Yes. Probably on his way here." Alexa's face was emotionless.

Langdon went back to the couch and sank down into it again. He leaned his head back, shut his eyes and placed his thumb and index finger on the pressure points located in his eyebrows.

"I heard he's the greatest hacker alive. He'll find us."

"He is pretty good, but I am better. Don't worry." She got up and plopped down on the couch next to him. "I have narrowed the person hunting me down to only one."

"How did you do that?"

She looked at him and he rolled his eyes, "Jeepers, I get it. Who then?"

"It's not any government. There has been no communication anywhere about me. It has to be the one person who has been behind the Salem Group in the shadows all along."

"Who?" He leaned forward, his body tense.

Alexa inhaled, "As far as I can trace, he is the benefactor who paid for all the research and activities of the group. No one knows who he is though, except Professor Li Geming."

Langdon's head jerked back, "Professor Li Geming! I know him. He and my dad go way back. They were together at the university."

"He is the one who initiated the Salem group. They were all students of his, years ago."

He shook his head, "It sounds like one of those conspiracy stories."

Alexa's shoulders slumped. "I wish it wasn't real but I'm living proof that they exist. I'm their project."

Awkwardly Langdon patted her shoulder, "Chin up, girl. We're going to win them. They can't get very far without you. So, who do you think the secret benefactor is?"

"There is only one man that had dealings with Professor Li Geming in the past that has the amount of money needed to fund this project. His name is Seth Hudson."

Langdon gave a low whistle "I've heard of him. He ranks as one of the richest men in the world." He tipped his head to the side, "He likes to keep a low profile, but I've never heard anything bad about him."

Alexa smiled at him, her eyes sparkling. "I think our pizza has arrived."

The intercom sounded and Langdon lifted one eyebrow at her before he went downstairs to collect it from the main entrance.

The aroma wafting up from the boxes made his mouth water. After fetching two glasses of water, they settled cross-legged on the grey laminate floor by the glass coffee table and tucked in. Alexa seemed to enjoy it as much as he did.

"You're staring at me."

Langdon felt himself blush. "Sorry, I didn't mean to." His brows pinched together, "How did you know about the pizza before the bell rung?"

He could see her mouth pucker as if she were hiding a grin. "I smelled it."

Both his eyebrows went up, his mouth agape, "From that

far away?"

"I have enhanced senses, but I can choose to activate them or not."

Langdon swallowed; his eyes locked with hers.

"You are staring again." Alexa took another piece of pizza.

"Darn it. I'm curious. Can you blame a guy?" *That and she was freakin' beautiful.*

"It's so easy to get taken in by outward appearances, isn't it."

Her blue eyes were looking at him solemnly. Before his astonished eyes, a mole grew as large as a bottle cap, on her cheek. It was hideous. She lifted her hand and covered it for a few seconds. When she took her hand away, flawless skin remained. A shiver went down his spine.

"Why did you do that?"

"To prove a point. You place too much value on what you see. It's the invisible that really matters."

Langdon blushed and stuffed his mouth with pizza. When he finished chewing, he asked, "These nanobots, why did they insert them in you? I don't get what they want you to do."

She took another pizza piece, "Take over the world. What else?"

He choked on the bite he was swallowing, "Seriously?"

"Salem stands for peace. They want a world of peace. A world not ruled by governments and the rich but by one fair entity. A world where drugs, alcohol, weapons and so forth aren't allowed."

Langdon stared at her with bulging eyes, "You. They want

you to rule the world?"

"Yip." Alexa avoided eye contact.

Langdon's mouth was dry and he licked his lips. "These nanobots. They can be programmed to do basically anything on an atomic level. I don't understand why my dad would give up such a ground-breaking technology to a group of fanatics."

His eyes grew large as he did a double take, "Do you realise that theoretically they could bring back the rain forest, eradicate world hunger. Make things that never wear out. I mean…Wow…No wonder they don't want anyone to know about it."

"In the wrong hands they can also destroy everything." Alexa softly uttered, her head bent.

Landon went on as if he hadn't heard her. "You're like a walking wonder. Can they extract the nanobots from you? Steal them so to speak? You'll never grow old or get sick." Langdon gulped; he couldn't get his head around it.

Alexa hesitated before she replied, "No. They are designed to function only in combination with my DNA. My clothes are really formed out of a combination of my DNA, nanobots and fibres. But if someone had the basic design, they should be able to modify it so that it can be programmed to do anything. When they leave my body they automatically self-destruct and if I should die, they'd self-destruct too." Her brows pulled in and her hand rubbed across her heart.

Langdon placed the last piece of gooey cheese into his mouth, he shook his head, "Why did my dad give it up?"

Alexa lowered the lid of the pizza box. "Your mom died around fourteen years ago, didn't she?"

"Yeah, a car accident. I don't remember anything. I

was only one." Langdon stared into Alexa's irises. A gasp escaped him and he gave her an incredulous stare, "You think they had something to do with it?"

She shook her head, "Not my parents or their friends, but Seth Hudson and Professor Li Geming might have organised it as a warning to your father to sign over the rights to his invention or else they'd kill you next and then him."

Langdon sat immobilized, his muscles rigid. The man who kidnapped his father might have killed his mother. "He's a monster!" His body started shaking, his breathing becoming erratic.

Alexa reached across the table for his hand. "I have this thing I do when my emotions feel too big for me." Softly she started humming. The vibration ran through her whole body into his. He took a deep breath and allowed it to sweep over him. Under his breath he started humming along. Within a few minutes the anger he felt dissipated.

He opened his eyes and stared wide-eyed at the water in his glass. It was swirling. Alexa's water was doing the same. The vibration of the humming seemed to have affected the water. She pressed his hand.

"The water likes it, just like the water in our bodies. The chaos gets restructured into harmony."

She picked up the glass and drank the water. He did the same, finding the taste sweeter with a less chorine-like aftertaste. Could frequency change water? He remembered watching YouTube videos on how frequency affects water years ago. Brain overload.

He crawled into bed feeling like he had run a marathon. Maybe these two days had been a bad dream and he would wake up back in his old bed with his dad making pancakes for breakfast tomorrow morning.

Sean McCutcheon sat licking an ice-cream in the park, enjoying the bright sunshine even though the temperature was below sixty-eight degrees Fahrenheit. That was spring for you, even in Berkeley. He thought back to the past two days and tried to make sense of it. His search of the lab had produced nothing. The professor wasn't working on anything to do with frequencies and there was no reference to Alexa and her parents. Mole had hacked into the computer and searched it high and low. Nothing.

Imagine his astonishment when he sat unobserved outside the building behind a newspaper and saw Alexa enter the building. She had a hoodie over her head but glanced towards the street and he recognised her. She left after half an hour as quietly as she came. He followed her to a mall where she met up with a blond-haired young man. They started shopping and looked for all the parts like teenagers in a mall. It made no sense. He had to buy himself a few items just to play the part.

Eventually they left and took a bus to an area on the other side of town, where they entered an apartment block. Sean waited outside and saw the pizza guy deliver their pizza. He itched to get a listening device inside, but caution kept him back. They still had no idea what abilities she had.

Along with that, the news that JJ had escaped from prison reached him as soon as the alarm was sounded. He'd placed a watch on that in case but was stunned that it happened. The man obviously had a plan. What was it?

Sean bit into the cone, chewing slowly. The facts. James and Ruth Johnson studied together, got married and had one daughter. Throughout the years they'd lived below the radar until a few months ago when JJ got caught after releasing sensitive data on the web. On the surface it had nothing to do with frequency. He took another bite, licking a drop of ice cream from his hand.

The whole reason Alexa came on their radar in the first place was because of a new system they were testing in airports. When Alexa walked past their scanner, her frequency was perfect. They had never had a reading like that before.

The list of things that brought people's frequency down causing disease was long and extensive; from coffee to alcohol to radiation from screens and pollution. Everything worked to keep people in a less-than-optimal estate. His bosses liked it that way. Sick people were their pots of gold.

He pushed the last bit of the cone in his mouth and wondered if he could allow himself another.

Sean got up and started strolling down the gravel path, his hands deep in his pockets and his head lowered. His mobile phone pinged and he read the text message, his face registering shock. *Carrie?*

James woke with a start in the dark. Instinctively his hand sought the pistol he had placed on the bedside table. All his senses were on high alert, his muscles taut. Ruth's gentle breathing could be heard from the single bed next to his.

She'd moved in under her single alias and he had snuck in without anyone seeing. Hopefully, they weren't looking so hard for a single woman. He laid back against the headboard, keeping the pistol on his lap, willing their invisible persecutors to show themselves. His hear trate returned to normal after a few minutes.

Getting up, he left the bedroom to the small open-plan

kitchen and living room their rental consisted of. The past day hadn't been very productive. The only thing they did find was Alexa's tracking chip, lying on the lab's tabletop. At least they knew she was there. After rooting through the lab's stuff, their only lead was a boy's skateboard, iPod and sports jacket that certainly didn't belong to Professor Anderson. According to the online information his son died seven years ago, but James knew Alexa could've manipulated the data. The footage of the lab was disrupted around the time they thought she was there until later.

He'd asked around and hit the jackpot with the blonde waitress across the road who knew the profs' son as Langdon. She had seen him leave the fast-food store with a brown-haired girl. The hair color meant nothing. The waitress noticed it because Langdon wasn't one who hung out with girls a lot. The time matched the arrival time at the lab recorded by her tracker, so it had to be Alexa. What did she want with the professor's son? James shut his eyes and scrubbed a hand over his face. He mentally went through the facts.

The professor and his son seemed to have disappeared, but the prof. didn't leave with Alexa. No one had seen him since yesterday. Where could Alexa be now? He opened his eyes and eyed his jacket hanging over the chair. Burning a hole in the side pocket was Alexa's letter. Pulling it out and sitting down on the chair, James stared at the single word on the front. Alexa never called him dad.

A memory came back to him. It had been a long day. He'd been working tirelessly to perfect the cooling system for the quantum computer. It was his invention that made the whole thing possible. He discovered that if they placed the system deep enough into the earth, the heat counterbalanced the extreme cold of the special nitrogen cooling system they installed around the processors. This made it possible for the screens to be placed nearby and bring humans into contact with it.

Something was off with the sensors which had taken him all day to fix. He stomped into the kitchen looking for food, late around nine p.m. He turned around and there was four-year-old Alexa standing watching him.

"Why aren't you sleeping?" He asked.

She came nearer and climbed onto the barstool by the kitchen island. "I'm not tired."

"I am tired and hungry." He blurted, before covering the sandwich he'd been making with mayonnaise and slapping on another slice of bread. He sat down and started munching on it. She stared at him with those disconcerting blue eyes.

"Do you love me?"

The unexpected question made him stop chewing. He closed his eyes to steal a moment to think.

"Of course I do. But you aren't just for me. You are for the whole world. It's my job to make sure they see that."

"So you work because you love me."

His throat thickened. "Something like that."

"Okay." She got up from the chair and left as still as she had come.

He stared after her remembering another little boy at the age of four.

"Daddy, you promised you'd play ball with me today." He stood in the doorway of his father's office at home with his bat and ball clutched in his hand.

His father didn't even look up from the papers he was

studying. "I'm sorry, son. Something has come up." To his assistant beside him he said, "Please find the gardener and ask him to play with James." The assistant walked over to James, placing her hand on his back.

As they walked out the door, she saw the tears pool in his eyes and said, "I'm sorry James. Your father works very hard so that you can have this large home and everything you can ask for."

He looked up at her, "So he chooses to work because he loves me?"

She bit her lip, "Something like that."

James shut the memory down. The pain was almost as fresh as if it was yesterday.

The single leaf of paper inside was handwritten.

'Dear Dad,

I'm sorry I've derailed your plans with me. I've simulated all the different outcomes of Salem's plan and none of them turn out well.

I've come to realise that transformation cannot come from the outside. It can only come from the inside. It cannot be forced.

Our house is compromised. Find out who bugged it. For your own safety. Please take care of

Mom. She needs you.

Love your daughter,

Lexi.'

His eyes lingered on the "love your daughter" part. He couldn't remember if she had ever said she loved him. No clues as to what she was planning. Of course she knew about the bugs. By now she probably knew who bugged it too. He didn't know how long he sat there mulling over her letter.

After working for it all his life, he couldn't believe what she said was true. None of the outcomes turned out well. Not one? He didn't want to believe her. But he knew that Alexa didn't lie and if anyone could almost work out the future, it was her. There must be a way to have Salem. The world needed peace! He scrunched up his face and released it a few times.

Her words kept repeating in his head. Transformation on the inside. It wasn't possible. The cynic in him wanted to scoff and rave at her words. People were products of nature. They either had a good hand dealt them with a personality that helped them get ahead, or not. Science was the only thing that could bring change. Alexa was a perfect example of that. She rebelled against Salem though. James tapped his fist against his lips. He had to talk to her.

His laptop beckoned to him. It took a matter of seconds to log onto his dark website. The one no one knew about except probably Alexa. Quickly, he typed a message and logged out again. Fingers crossed she would make contact.

"Oscar White I'm counting to three. If you don't come down from that treehouse right now, you'll be in trouble young man!"

A scrambling could be heard before two thin white legs dangled down the ladder. Oscar ran to his mother who was standing with her hands on her wide hips behind the house.

"I'm sorry, Mom."

"Your breakfast is getting cold, what time did you get up anyhow? I had a mild shock to find your bed empty. Did you sleep up there?" She peered at him through narrowed eyes.

"No, Mom. I woke up with this urgency to pray for Alexa and her family. I think they're in trouble."

His mom's posture relaxed, and she patted him on the shoulder, "You're a good boy, my son."

Inclining her head, she said, "I tell you what, you go back to your praying and I'll bring you a few supplies for the stomach. If the good Lord tells you to do something, He usually has a very good reason for it."

Oscar startled her with a kiss on the lips, "Thanks, Mom."

She watched as he ran back to the tree house and sent up a silent prayer for them herself. Strength in numbers and all that. She'd only met Alexa once and liked what she saw. A bit strange, but kind-hearted girl. It was quite a shock to see how their house had imploded. Not a usual occurrence, houses collapsing. Someone wanted to take them out. She shook her head in disbelief. These things didn't happen in their neighbourhood.

The sleeping form of the teenage boy stirred a bit before snoozing off again. The light from the window irritated his eyelids. Turning his face away, he muttered something in his sleep before rolling over on his back. Focusing on the ceiling, the strange surroundings roused him fully to consciousness.

A quick consult of his wristwatch confirmed that breakfast would almost be lunch. Then he remembered the girl in the other room and his instincts were fully aware. Hastily throwing clothes on, he tried to appear nonchalant as he entered the living room.

Alexa was standing in the kitchen with a pan holding a sizzling omelette.

She greeted him with a smile. "Almost ready."

He stifled a yawn and sat down at the island on the barstool. "Good morning. Did you sleep well?" Does she sleep, he wondered uneasily. There was too much he didn't know about her.

Alexa slipped the omelette onto a plate that she placed in front of him. "You can trust me. That's the most important thing isn't it?"

The pupils in his green irises widened, "Do you read minds?"

She giggled, "I would love to, but no. I'm just very good at reading body language."

Langdon squinted at her, "You mean that malarkey about eighty percent communication is body language?"

"Something like that, yes."

Alexa sat down opposite him, with her own omelette. The smell of fried bacon and mushrooms wafted off their plates. They ate, both lost in their thoughts.

"One question." Her blue eyes twinkled with mischief.

He rolled his eyes, "Almost sounds like you could be a genie and I have three wishes. I should ask what number the jackpot is going to be."

Her face remained completely deadpan and he quirked his eyebrow, "You actually know that?" He took another bite chewing over what to ask.

"Are you happy?"

Her fork paused halfway to her mouth before lowering down to the plate. She stared at him; a puzzled frown etched on her forehead.

"No one's asked me that before."

He broke her stare and looked at his plate, "Last thing my dad asked me. It just came back to me as rather an important question."

A slender hand reached over the counter and touched the top of his hand briefly. "Thank you."

He hesitated, "Are you?" After a few seconds he sought her eyes and to his dismay found tears there. "I'm sorry!" He sprang up, went round the counter and hugged her to him. For a moment she was nothing but a normal teenage girl in trouble. Her arms went round his and they stood there for a little while. His shoulder sported a small wet patch when they let go of each other.

Langdon brushed his fringe to the side. "As you can see, I'm a bit awkward around girls. Home-schooled and all that. I've never made one cry."

"It's not you. I don't normally cry. My happiness has just never mattered. All that matters is the cause."

"Surely it has to matter somewhat. I mean, what good is a worthy cause if you're unhappy?"

"I'm happy this moment if that matters." Alexa blurted out, her voice inflecting more than usual and a healthy red blush spreading on her cheeks.

Langdon grinned his own cheeks flushing. "Cool."

They cleaned up the kitchen and then Langdon went out to the shops for some more supplies. It took him longer than he thought, and he grabbed some takeout for a late lunch. The moment he entered the flat, he knew she wasn't there. The note on the low table in the living room beckoned him. Scanning it quickly he clenched his jaw and checked his watch. She couldn't be far away, but without knowing which park she was heading to there was no way he could find her.

Memorizing the address she had given him, he destroyed the note. Next, he packed up the few items he possessed including the new passport she got him. They picked it up yesterday from a drop point. There was no doubt in his mind that it hadn't come through proper channels but who was he to complain? He had to find his father. It looked like she had disabled the laptop. No one would be able to find anything on there. So that was that.

Pacing up and down, he checked his watch every five minutes. He didn't know God but given the few options left he decided to cover every base and sent up a small prayer. "Please protect Alexa and help me find my dad." His restlessness subsided and he sat down.

On the other side of town, Alexa had slipped into the park with her white hoodie over her head and dark glasses on. The park had high black iron fences on top of a low brick wall all around with open gates at every entrance. The sun was shining brightly on the first day of April. Unusually warm for spring. The bare tall beech trees were starting to form bright green leaves. She walked along the pedestrian- and cyclist-only pathway until she reached the right bench. She was five minutes early for her meeting with her dad.

Sitting down on the cold, black-painted iron slats, she tuned into her surroundings. Nothing unusual in a mile radius. She could hear no one talking secretly on any frequency. As her dad entered the park from the opposite side, she picked him up noting nothing hidden on his person. She slipped her sunglasses off and threw her hoodie back.

In her hand she had something invisible, she had made in Professor Anderson's lab. She went there the previous day; confident they weren't watching it at that moment. As soon as her dad sat down next to her, she brushed his hand sending her invisible tracker nanobot into his skin. It had to be programmed to match his DNA, which she did by using a carefully kept strand of his hair. Only she could access it if she needed to find him.

"Hi, Dad."

He stirred but didn't reprove her, "Hi, Alexa."

"I'm glad you are out."

"Not by choice." At this, he looked at her and she gazed back into his eyes searchingly.

"Have you questioned how much you really do by choice?"

He squinted and tilted his head, "Philosophical now, are we?"

"Do you remember how you were recruited by Professor Li Geming."

James sighed looking down at his lap, "Why dredge up the past?"

Alexa sat with her shoulders back, "Do you still believe it was chance that he chose you along with the others? You were specifically targeted. He studied everything about you and used it to his advantage. Your relationship with your parents, your desire to prove yourself, your need to feel that you are making a difference." Her voice was low-pitched and steady, her gaze alert on him.

The man who fathered her stiffened, "I've always felt

honoured that he chose me. I still do."

She nodded, "That is because he wanted you to feel that way. He portrayed the father figure you craved."

"Bull." His hand wiped across his face. "Your mother is very worried about you. Won't you come with me and we can discuss this in a more secure environment."

Alexa looked down at her lap, "Professor Anderson has been kidnapped. I believe the people hunting us are being paid by Seth Hudson. He is the money backer of the Salem group."

"All the more reason for us to stick together." He was pleading.

She shook her head, "I might endanger you more. Promise me you will take care of Langdon Anderson, the professor's son, if something happens to me."

James took her hand, their slender fingers entwined. "Alexa, Lexi, are you sure? None of the outcomes?" His voice trailed off, still laced with disbelief.

"I'm sorry. None. Real transformation can never happen from the outside-in. It will create other problems, bigger problems. How can you justify killing everyone who doesn't comply? You would be worse than the worst dictators in history. None of them created the perfect world of peace you hunger after."

"We won't kill them. We'll reprogram them." His voice had risen in volume.

"Listen to yourself, Dad. It sounds like you are talking about machines." Alexa countered calmly.

James held himself rigid before slumping down and giving a self-deprecating laugh. "I'd hoped I could talk some sense into you."

Alexa shifted nearer to him and rested her head on his shoulder. James stared down at the top of her head and lightly kissed the top of it. He wanted to tell her he loved her, but the words choked in his throat. How do you start being a normal dad if all you've ever been is a man focused on a goal who used his own daughter as a means to an end?

"I forgive you, Dad."

He felt the wetness on his cheeks. He didn't deserve her.

"I'll take care of Langdon."

She left without another word and he fought every instinct that screamed to not let her go. A cloud moved in front of the sun and he got off the bench, walking the opposite way with legs feeling like lead. His throat felt thick and his chest tight. There had to be another solution, but Alexa would've thought of all the possibilities. The thoughts in his head felt muddled and his lips pressed together in a grimace.

Alexa was distracted as she came near the exit gate of the park, working through the complex emotions surging through her. When she felt the pinprick that went straight through her hoodie and T-shirt into her stomach, it took a millisecond to recognise that she was under attack.

Even as every single thing in her started fighting against the strong surge of sedative invading her body, she lost the battle quickly before everything shut down. The quantity of sedative was enough to bring down an elephant. They had accurately guessed that her nanobots would not be able to combat it fast enough, but only lessen it to the point where it didn't kill her.

CHAPTER 4

Langdon consulted his watch again. Time was up. Alexa's letter said that if she didn't come back before four p.m., he should go to the address she had provided and meet with her parents. His palms sweated as he locked the flat and hurried along the corridor. It took him less than half an hour to reach the place. He was glad they got him a new skateboard yesterday.

Near the address he slowed down and got off. A man and woman came out of the brick apartment building. The man looked familiar and as he neared them, the blue eyes of the woman matched Alexa's although less bright.

He accosted them. "Are you Alexa's parents?"

The man didn't look surprised, but simply said, "You must be Langdon."

The woman looked at the man, "You know him?"

"He's Professor Anderson's son. The professor's been kidnapped."

"Do you know where Alexa is?" Langdon inserted impatiently. Something pinged on the sidewalk next to them and Langdon's breath

hitched. "Someone's shooting at us!"

"Come on!" James grabbed them both and jostled a man who was getting into a yellow taxi in front of them out of the way. "Sorry, we're in a hurry." The glass of the lamppost shattered above them as they dove into the taxi. James pulled out a wad of cash and threw it at the driver. "Get us to the airport pronto." The man didn't have to be asked twice but floored the accelerator.

Ruth was gripping James' hand in a death grip. "Do you think they'll follow us?"

James glanced out the back window. "I don't think so. They staked out the apartment, but I don't think they expected us to make a run for it."

"What about my stuff?"

"Forget it, I have our passports and money. We'll be fine."

Ruth retracted into herself, letting go of his hand.

"Have you got a passport?" James shot off towards Langdon.

"Alexa got me one."

"Where is she?" Ruth straightened up, bending forward to see Langdon around James.

"Ask him!" Langdon pointed at James. "She told me to meet you if she doesn't come back after her meeting with Dad here."

"I don't know! She left the park in the opposite direction at two o'clock." James fisted his hands, releasing a pent-up breath.

"You— Ruth's face was turning red.

James held up his hands, "—I couldn't take you with me. She was never going to come back with me, and you couldn't handle that."

"Who are you to decide what I can and can't do?" Ruth ground out. "What if it was the last time we ever saw her James. Did you think of that?"

"I don't know!" He shouted. "Stop accusing me! I did what I thought was best at the time. She's protecting us by going into hiding. Maybe she's just gone underground again after securing our protection of Langdon here."

"She asked you to look after me?" Langdon frowned. Why deviate from the plan? There was so much that he didn't understand. Wasn't he safer at the flat under his fake name than with her parents who were being hunted by the goons sent after them? His mind flipped back to him offering her his help and it dawned on him that maybe she wanted him to help her parents while she followed another lead.

"Listen, do you have a plan?" This he directed to James, since Ruth had turned away from them staring through the window at the gray blur of the city going by. The driver was earning his money and exceeding the speed limit to get them to the airport.

James' voice was low and strained, "The only option left is to visit The Facility. At least then we can know if she is safe and contact her."

Langdon inclined his head, "The Facility? Does Seth Hudson know where this place is?"

"Only the Salem group knows."

"So Professor Li Geming knows too?" Langdon's question hung in the air the implication clear.

"He would never betray us, we're his protégés. He basically birthed the Salem group." It didn't sound as convincing as James meant it. Who else could give away their locations? One of the others? His stomach felt rock hard, his chest paining.

Christine Palmer was pacing up and down the nondescript living room of the apartment they had hastily rented under one of their aliases. It wasn't that far from their previous hide-out, but far enough to be safe. Her colorful trousers that flared out below her knees complemented her layered white top.

"I'm telling you Evan, it's those teenage hormones. Alexa isn't acting rationally."

Evan was reclining on the low, sagging brown couch. Where his wife was tall and thin, he was short and round.

He shifted on the couch and sunk deeper in. "Calm down,

Christine. You know last month's tests showed that she was keeping her hormones as balanced as a hover board. She even paused her periods."

His wife threw her hands in the air, her voice shrill, "Why then I ask you, why? Now we are being hunted by who knows who and she blew our plan sky-high, less than a month before D-Day."

"Come sit down, Christine, you are making me nervous."

She stomped over to him and nestled down next to him, pulling her legs onto the couch. His arm went around her shoulders and she pressed into him.

"I'm scared, Evan, it wasn't supposed to happen like this."

"I know honey, but we'll be okay. James and Ruth will find a way and before you know it everything will be back on track." They sat mulling it over. Evan cleared his throat, "You know, the more I think about it, I think Alexa knew the houses were being bugged. She was bound to pick it up."

"Why didn't she just warn us?"

"I think she knew that whoever it was, was connected to us in some way. She needed to get out to expose the traitor in our midst."

At this Christine pulled back to look at him, "Really? A traitor?" She shook her head, "I can't think anyone could betray our cause. We are a small group after all."

"It might be money. Can you imagine how much we could make if we programmed nanobots that would help women to control their periods?"

A smile flittered across her face, "I'd sign up myself." She sighed and rested her head down on his shoulder again. "All

I want to do is escape to our dream island and live the rest of our lives in peace.

"Soon, honey. Just a few years, and this world won't be recognizable. Then we can retire knowing we changed the world for the better." His gaze darted down to her.

"My head aches." Christine closed her eyes.

"Mine too." He leaned back onto the couch. "Let's take a nap."

They fell asleep unaware of the canister of carbon monoxide underneath the couch, controlled by the man parked in the blue car across the road. After checking with his binoculars through their front window and seeing them asleep, he pressed the control button and opened it fully. Within five minutes Evan and Christine Palmer, two of the brilliant biotechnicians of the Salem group were in this world no more.

Alexa never dreamed. It was one of those strange side effects of being permanently connected to the most advanced quantum computer in the world. So when she opened her eyes and found herself sitting on a wooden bench next to a river, she knew that something strange was going on. It felt real but it couldn't be just like when you dreamed. There was something weird about the way she felt too. Her mind was empty. No multiple solutions of every possible outcome were streaming through her in the background. There were no electron pulses to detect. Nothing.

She concentrated on influencing her nanobots to see if she could grow the mole she had made to prove a point to Langdon, and nothing happened. Did they remove them? Was she in some kind of virtual world, maybe? Being tricked into a false sense of safety. The world didn't strike her as normal. She felt more human than usual but all around her, there was an intensity of life that wasn't apparent on earth.

There was a splash in the river, and she noticed a silverfish heading upstream. The water was crystal clear reflecting the colorful stones on the riverbed. She tracked the slow progress of the fish, marvelling at its perseverance. Going against the stream.

"Courageous, isn't he?" The voice out of nowhere startled her. It sounded close.

"Where am I?" Alexa was distracted by the sound of her voice. It sounded richer and warmer.

"The men who kidnapped you are transporting you to Seth Hudson's estate in the south but I've translocated you into my kingdom's realm."

Alexa tittered. For some inexplicable reason she found it funny. The laughter kept bubbling up till she gave in and bellowed aloud till the tears streamed down her cheeks. She'd laughed herself off the bench and was lying on her back on the soft green grass. The blue sky above her was luminous with purple clouds drifting lazily across it. She inhaled the scent of honey blossoms and felt more relaxed than she'd ever been before. Maybe they'd given her a drug.

"Who are you?" She lazily thought.

The reply was a gentle wind that came out of nowhere and blew over her, rustling through the grass, and the tree behind the bench.

She took a deep breath, breathing in the wind and felt as if it invaded her, expanding into every corner.

"El." She said it without thinking. It felt right.

"I am." The wind gently played with her hair, "Who are you, Alexa?"

In that moment she felt so at peace that her response was again without thought, "I am a human being."

It felt like the wind was chortling as it caressed her face, "And what is a human being, dear Alexa?"

She sat up and studied her hands, tracing the lines across her palm, "We are a mystery. At face value just flesh and bone, with a soul somewhere, but so much more somehow."

"Those that say you are inferior exasperate you?"

Alexa nodded, "Even if you are stupid or ugly, there is something about humans that is special. I don't think we are equal to animals somehow."

"You are perceptive."

Alexa sat up, trailing her fingers through the grass. "I like it here."

"This is home. Where you were before you went to earth." The wind seemed to form a window in front of her in mid-air; the scenery through the window shifted as a myriad of dimensions flipped past.

Alexa sat slack-jawed, drinking in the beauty and mystery of the scenes. The wind dropped away, and the air hung heavy around her.

"El?" She whispered.

"Alexa?" The still, quiet voice was near her.

"Why are humans special?"

"Breathe."

She took a deep breath and the wind invaded her like before, until it felt like every cell in her body absorbed it. The feeling coursing through her was one of wild ecstasy. As she exhaled, she released a sound similar to someone on a roller coaster. She ran in circles, whooping, roaring and howling all at once. Spent, she flopped down on the grass again.

The wind whispered in her ear, "Humans are the only beings who I inhabit."

"You…" The thought of who He was seemed to overwhelm her.

"Me in you."

"Me in You?" Alexa's eyes roved around her.

"In Me."

"All this is in You, but all that You are can be in me?" She had a feeling that even if she were connected to her AI self, she wouldn't be able to comprehend it.

"But how?"

"I made a way for you through the blood of my Son. Through Him you have access."

Alexa's heart thudded. "It's true? He is the way, the truth and the life?"

"Yes. If you choose to receive Him, you receive everlasting life." The wind caressed her face. She closed her eyes. "I don't understand."

"You will. Faith brings understanding." The wind dropped away. In the lull, his soft voice spoke, "Do you want to see Salem?" At this strange request, Alexa stood up. All around her was nature as far as she could see.

"Yes?" The words had barely left her lips, before the wind started whirling around her, faster and faster till it lifted her up. It felt like a fun ride on a merry-go-round. Alexa shut her eyes, whooping exuberantly. She didn't know what would happen next and it didn't matter. She could trust Him.

The air became brighter and she glimpsed something below. The wind descended with her until she stood on a translucent road in the middle of a city like none on earth.

On her way over she had glimpsed its form resembling a cube, with three gates on each side formed out of gigantic pearls. Everything from the roads to the buildings was made of gold, so pure it was almost transparent. Beneath her, through the road she caught the reflection of the purple amethyst foundation, which was the top layer of a twelve-layered foundation, made up of different precious stones.

The abundance of materials which were sought after and coveted by people on earth astounded her. All the riches of the earth couldn't even build a small portion of this city.

"It's so beautiful." Alexa sighed.

"There is no pain, no weeping, no hungry or thirsty in this city. Only the pure, redeemed, forgiven people of the Way will be allowed into it."

Alexa turned wide blue eyes to the sky, where for the first time, she noticed there was no sun, although everything was bathed in a warm light.

"My family wants this peace on earth. They've devoted their lives to it."

The gentle caress of the wind blew around her, "I know my child. But their desire is perverted. The only way to bring peace to the earth is to find My peace. To find the Way."

"Through your Son?"

"Yes." The wind picked her up and within seconds she was hovering above the earth with its green and blue, beautiful form seen below her.

"I love the earth and its inhabitants. I have good plans for it. You are part of it. I'm going to send you to someone whom I've chosen to help you. Stay with him until I bring you back to your time."

Before she could ask another question, she felt herself fall asleep.

Sean hovered outside the hospital room. He'd had his hand on the handle twice now without going in. He hadn't seen Carrie in thirty years. Memories of them as children surfaced in him. Carrie and him playing in the park. Hiding in the cupboard when their dad was in a drunken state.

The last time he'd seen her they'd had a massive quarrel. She was heading off with a few losers and all his pleading didn't help. First, there were a few postcards as she travelled across the states, the last one from Las Vegas. Then they stopped. It was part of what motivated him to become a detective.

His hand took hold of the silver handle again. Resolutely he pushed it down and entered the room. Nothing could prepare him for the sight. She lay small and frail in the white bed. Her dark hair was plastered against her head looking brittle. The yellow tint of her skin diminished the attractiveness of her face. Her dark eyes fluttered open and she stared at him.

"Sean?" her hoarse voice whispered.

"Carrie?" He stepped up to the bed, taking her hand in his.

"Sean." She sighed as if a burden had lifted off her shoulders.

"What's going on?"

"I'm dying."

"Why?"

She chortled, "That's my brother, always after the facts."

He pressed her hand tighter, "Can't they do something?"

Her voice was low and strained, "I have idiopathic aplastic anemia."

"What does that mean?"

"My bone marrow is damaged, so my body stopped producing new blood cells."

"I can give you blood."

"Not going to help, little bro." She seemed out of breath.

"How did you get it?" His heart was thudding in his chest. This wasn't the sister he remembered. She was a shell of herself.

"I got lupus, but I didn't know it. So tired all the time." Her voice faltered.

"It triggered the anaemia."

Sean realized that there were tears dripping down his cheeks. "I looked for you all these years."

She'd closed her eyes but opened them again to look at him. "I know. I'm sorry. My life was a mess. I didn't want to drag you into it."

"I missed you." He didn't recognise his own voice. "Now I'm going to lose you again?"

"I love you, little bro." Her eyes fluttered shut.

A nurse came in, checked the drips and monitors. She indicated that he should follow her out.

"You're her next of kin, right?"

"Yes. Her brother."

"Can you please sign some paperwork for me?" Mutely he followed her down the corridor to the nurses' station. On autopilot, he filled out the form with his details. When he came to the payment details, he gingerly signed his name too. Moving the papers across the desk he caught the eye of the nurse, noticing her blue eyes for the first time.

"Who brought her in? Has anyone been visiting?"

"No one that I know of. She walked into the emergency room two days ago and collapsed before we could see her. She had your number clutched in her hand." She gave him a sympathetic smile.

"Isn't there any treatment for her condition?" Involuntarily he held his breath.

The nurse avoided eye contact, "Bone marrow transplant might work, but often doesn't. We've started giving her auto-immune drugs." She mentioned a figure for the bone transplant and his mouth went dry. Even if he sold his house, he couldn't generate that sum.

Sean clenched his jaw. "Thank you."

She gave him a comforting smile and left. Sean made his way down the hallway again. By Carrie's door he leaned back against the wall. The helplessness wasn't a feeling he welcomed. He hugged his shoulders, his chin resting on his chest. There had to be something he could do. Alexa's perfect features and frequency came to mind. What if she had a technology that could heal? It felt like a jolt went through him. He straightened his shoulders and looked at the door of Carrie's hospital room. "I'm going to find help. Don't give up, Carrie."

He started for the elevator, hurrying. He didn't have much time. The hospital was in New York and Alexa was back in Berkeley.

The blue van disguised as part of an electrical company's fleet reached the private home in the Los Altos Hills in California in a little over an hour. They pulled into the garage without anyone noticing them.

In the back of the van, they had secured their package in a specially designed box. It was almost like a miniature Faraday cage. No signals could go in or out of it. It was also reinforced with a bulletproof glass lid, reinforced titanium sides and a special mechanical locking mechanism which kept it locked and sealed. The air vents were tiny, all around the lid.

Whoever had designed it knew exactly what type of prisoner it was going to contain. The men slid the box out of the dark interior of the van and almost dropped it in their shock. The glare of the electric lights showed the inside of the box empty as if they had never made the trip to grab the girl.

They stared at each other in frozen silence, mentally rehearsing their trip. They'd switched vehicles and secured her in the box after which they drove straight here. At no point did she have a chance to escape. The door between the house and the garage opened and their captain indicated to them that they should slide the box back into the truck.

The man who entered the garage walked up to the tall captain dressed in black and barked, "Package secure?"

"Yes, Sir." He stared into the dark eyes unflinchingly.

"Good." The man nodded. "You can transport her to the

containment room and leave her in the box there.”

He turned around and left without glancing at the truck again. A collective sigh went up from the men after he left.

The shortest one of them, with his bare head freshly shaven said, “Captain, what are we going to do?”

His captain stared at the van door, “Shortie if I were a believing man, I’d pray for that darn girl to reappear. As I’m not, I’d say we deliver the box, and disappear. Maybe if we lay low in South America for a while, his boss won’t find us.”

Another one of the men who had a scar across his cheek said, “Couldn’t we explain what happened?”

The Captain walked over to him, placing his hand on the man’s shoulder, “We could, and he might even believe us. But I know his type. He’ll kill us just because he’s angry that his plan isn’t going to plan. Do any of you want to take that risk?”

As one they shook their heads. Covering up the box with a piece of material they had in the van, they strode like coffin bearers to the set-apart containment area, where they left the box on top of a stainless-steel table in the empty room.

Once out of it, the door automatically locked behind them. They hastened to the van and escaped from the estate as quickly as possible. They didn’t relax until they were far away. How did she escape? It filled more than one of the men with a sense of inexplicable fear. Like a magic trick you couldn’t explain. It simply wasn’t humanly possible.

They tried to rest on the flight to New York. Thanks to the time difference it was already late in the night by the time they left the airport in a plain navy, Toyota saloon rental.

James missed the Cadillac he had to leave in Berkeley.

"I'm sorry to do this to you, Langdon, but you need to be blindfolded for the rest of this trip."

"But it's dark outside."

"It doesn't matter. You can't even have a vague idea of where The Facility is."

Begrudgingly, Langdon took the blindfold from James and put it on. Ruth tuned the radio onto a popular New York station. She hadn't spoken one word to either of them the whole trip. Her frosty silence chilled the air even though the music crammed it with noise.

They drove for an hour and it was approaching midnight when they turned off into an industrial area. Here, all the large buildings seemed alike. James pulled in behind one of them, taking care to hide the car behind a bush.

Langdon wanted to pull off the blindfold but James hissed that he should keep it on, grabbing his arm and leading him across the parking lot into the one next to them.

They slowly crept across two more parking lots before they waited in the shadows of the building. It was quiet. An owl hooted from the woods behind the fence at the back. James hurried them to the gray metallic door in the middle of the square double-story. As soon as they stood in front of it, it noiselessly slid open allowing them entry before sliding shut behind them again.

Langdon had become quite disorientated by now and was relieved to feel the blindfold being removed although it remained pitch dark. A small torch came to light in James' hand and they followed the beam along the corridor to where an elevator light blinked. There weren't any buttons. It opened in front of them as if on autopilot and whisked them down underneath the building. They stepped out of it into a small room which lit up with a red light that moved over them like a scanner.

James cleared his throat, "Whatever you see today, you can never ever repeat to anyone. Understood?" His eyes were dark, his stance unmoving.

Langdon nodded, wide-eyed. No one would believe him anyway. The door on the other side of the small room opened and they stepped out into a vast room with sleek-looking walls except for the one which was one large screen.

"Hello Alexa," James said and the screens lit up with the face of Lexi smiling at them. "Hello, James, Ruth and Langdon. Glad to see you. Something is wrong with my human."

Three chairs appeared out of the floor, and they sat down in them facing the screen.

Langdon had gone very pale and used a shaky hand to move his unruly fringe away.

"Could we see what you see at the moment?" James asked.

The screen turned black. "She's been unconscious since five minutes past two p.m. yesterday. The only input is her heart beating and her breathing. The outer senses are shut down."

Ruth released the breath she'd been holding. "Alexa, show us the last five minutes before she went unconscious."

The screen split up into smaller ones, the middle one showed the park. There was the sound of traffic and a lone bird in the background. Another screen showed all the electromagnetic spots in a mile radius around her. A fourth screen showed a camera from a building across the street which showed Alexa step out of the gate, her hoodie covering her head.

The middle screen showed how she looked down at her stomach, her hand clutching at a small red dart sticking out of her hoodie. The screen showing the visual input dimmed and went black. The camera on the building showed her collapsing.

A navy van parked down the road started up, roared up the few meters, braked while two men with ski masks jumped out the back and grabbed Alexa. On another screen, a strange bunch of little machines resembling bees were attacking the drug she had been injected with, but soon all motion stopped, and they looked like bees that had been smoked, all sleepy.

James let an expletive escape his lips before saying, "Have you traced the van?"

The screens showed the route of the van through various cameras, until it left the city. "I haven't picked it up again along the routes it could take. It doesn't show on any cameras."

Langdon spoke, finding his throat dry, "They must have had a second vehicle stashed."

"Yes. They did the same with your dad."

"Any more information on Seth Hudson?" James' voice had taken on a hard quality and his body was tense.

"I've found the money route from him to Professor Li Geming. It was very well hidden."

"Are our aliases still safe?"

"Yes."

"Can you book us flights to China and accommodation

for tonight?"

"China!" Langdon exclaimed. "I've got to stay here and find my dad."

James turned to him, "I think the only way to get to him would be to go see our friend Professor Li Geming. He's the leader of our group and if Seth Hudson is hunting us, he'll help us stop him."

"Why would he support us all these years and suddenly turn against us?" Ruth questioned.

"There are only a few logical reasons." Alexa answered. "Either he has changed his mind about the Project and doesn't want Salem anymore, which seems unlikely. Or he suspects us of not wanting to comply and has a backup plan to bring Salem about, which he is now implementing. In order to do that, though, he has to erase the Salem group."

Ruth sat up straighter, "Can you check up on Evan and Christine for me? I haven't been able to reach them."

Alexa was quiet for two minutes, "There hasn't been any activity at their house since yesterday, but they haven't left it. I've alerted the emergency services. They will be there in five minutes."

"Maybe they're sleeping, and we'll be on their radar for nothing," James grumbled.

They could hear the radio crackle as the ambulance reported that they were on their way. The silence was tense, and Langdon focused on settling his breathing. *Was his dad still alive? What were they going to do to Alexa? Why was this computer linked to her in such a personal way? Was she an AI or human? Or both?* These thoughts didn't help, so he stared at the white tiled floor wondering absently who kept it so spotless.

A radio crackled again and they could hear one of the members of the response team coughing. "We have a situation here. It looks like suicide or accidental death. I think it's carbon monoxide. We will need protective gear to remove the male and female bodies inside.

Ruth had sucked in her breath; her hands were shaking as she covered her face. "No, oh no, not Evan and Christine." Her anguished sobs echoed in the room. Alexa's face came back on the screen.

"I am sorry."

"It's not your fault, Alexa." James spoke quietly. "We knew there were risks with our plan."

He paused, "If Seth Hudson is behind this, he might have planned this as an option from the start. And if he is such a cold-hearted killer, who says he wouldn't have simply eliminated us further down the road, after Salem was established." His hands were clammy.

Lowering his voice, he said, "I have a feeling he's a man who likes to be in control."

"Are you telling me that we've been inadvertently working for this man all this time? The very type of dictator that we want to eliminate? The embodiment of everything we hate about corrupt governments and men seeking power instead of helping the people?" Ruth's voice had risen hysterically. She threw her hands in the air, "How did you not know this? Why didn't you check where the money came from?"

"I trusted Professor Li!" James shouted, his nostrils flaring.

Ruth stood up facing him, her body taut, and in a low voice said, "And I trusted you."

James flinched and she missed the anguish crossing his

face as she turned towards Alexa.

"Alexa, will you please log that I'm done with the Salem group. From now on I only want to be Lexi's mother and I'm going to spend the rest of my life trying to help her live it as normally and happily as she can."

"Ruth!" James shocked voice echoed through the room.

Her shoulders hunched and she looked down, "I'm done, James. If you're not, that's your business but I've given up enough for a cause that I don't believe in anymore. I'm taking Alexa back. She does not belong to the group anymore. You will have her over my dead body." Her hands were in fists, as she squared her shoulders and lifted her head.

James gaped at her back, astonished that the quiet, compliant, pretend wife he'd had for fourteen years could even say such things. It had to be the shock of losing their friends. She'd come round again, wouldn't she? And what would he do if she didn't? He couldn't even contemplate that.

Addressing Alexa again, Ruth enquired, "Have you checked and warned the others?"

"I have. They read the message, so they are still safe."

Langdon couldn't stop the yawn that escaped him which reminded everyone that it was past midnight.

"You have to go." Alexa's voice sounded sad.

James cleared his throat, "You know what to do if your protocols get breached. Your escape route is secure, and I'll build you into a new system as soon as everything is safe. Be careful. We don't know if there might not be..." His sentence trailed off.

They trooped out of the room, Langdon giving the screen

one last longing look, blushing as Alexa winked at him, before fading from view. They went through the secure room, up in the elevator and were back in their rental car before long.

James had placed the blindfold back on Langdon before they left the building. Ruth's phone beeped and she showed James the hotel address Alexa had booked for them. They needed their sleep. In a few hours, they would be in the air on their way to China.

If whoever was hunting them didn't find them first.

CHAPTER 5

Christopher galloped out of the wooden gates; his cheeks flushed with angry red spots accentuating his narrow face. His blue eyes, normally so placid, had sparks of lightning shooting from them. He hated them. The whole lot of them.

He fumed as he urged his black mare along the stony road. She seemed to tap into his anger, snorting and bringing her hooves down hard as she ran. Instinctively he headed for one of his haunts where he went for solace.

After an hour and a half, their mad speed had simmered down to a canter. The welcome green clifftops appeared. Dismounting, he left her halter loose for her to graze, knowing she wouldn't stray far. The anger had turned into despondence. His mouth was downturned, his breathing shallow.

He approached the sheer drop, where he threw himself to the ground as near to the dangerous edge as he could. Why didn't he just go over it? No one would miss him. A cold shiver ran through his tall frame, and he pulled

his knees under his chin, circling them with his arms. There had to be a reason for his miserable existence, but in the past eighteen years, he hadn't discovered it. It surely wasn't to be the next great knight, like his father. He rubbed his forearms.

The fencing lesson he had just run from came back to him. The burning blows of his opponent still smarted on his body. The tips were covered, but they left bruises. His instructor had never watered down his opinion; Christopher was the worst student he had ever had unlike his adopted brother, Godwin.

Thoughts of Godwin brought another type of blush to his cheeks. Godwin, as tall as himself, but with muscles in all the right places, agile, a born athlete. He'd always bested him at everything, but mercifully he didn't rub it in. His parents had adopted Godwin after his parents died when he was young. He was one of the few people who actually encouraged

Christopher. He hugged himself tighter, his cheeks burning. If Godwin knew what Christopher felt for him, he'd probably run for the hills.

The sound of the waves crashing far below reached him and he drew in a few deep breaths of the salty sea air. The gray, overcast sky matched his mood. Crossing his legs, he tried to empty his mind and tune into his surroundings. A seagull screeched overhead, the wind picked up and blew a few strands of his long brown hair out of its band. He loosened it, and let the wind blow his locks to its heart's content.

A dull thud penetrated his focus on nothing. There, it sounded again, far below. Puzzled, he opened his eyes and carefully lay down on his stomach, clutching the grass as he tried to look over the edge. Far below there was a small cove, and at low tide, like now, there was a tiny beach that could be reached via a steep path. Whatever it was thudded twice.

Christopher got up, brushing off his brown tunic and stood undecided, but curiosity got the better of him. With long strides he walked along the cliff to where the path started and as quickly as he safely could, he made his way down. The wind buffeted him and his hand scraped against the granite while he kept as near to the rock facade as possible. The thud reached his ears again, louder this time. The path rounded the cliffs before it leveled down to the small patch of sand.

He rubbed his hand across his face, wondering if he was hallucinating. Gently drifting in the water was a large box. It was shaped in a rectangle about six feet long, two feet wide and deep. The metal was unlike anything he had ever seen, it shimmered even though there was no sunlight. The water nudged it towards the shore and it banged against an outcrop of rock.

As Christopher stepped onto the sand to cross the distance towards the box, he felt his chest tighten, his stomach was in knots. He could leave now. Pretend he didn't see it. His steps slowed and he glanced over his shoulder, but he ignored his inner voice and kept moving towards the curious thing in the water. Grabbing hold of the thinner end nearest to him, he pulled it towards the sand, until he had it safely out of the water. His hands were green, for slimy algae covered it. Wiping his fingers across the top of it, his breath left his lungs in a whoosh.

He couldn't stop staring into the box, for the lid was transparent and inside lay a person. Panic made his hands tremble as he looked for a lever or catch to open up the box. *What if she is dead?* His slender fingers felt all along the sides, until they came across a mechanism. He pulled at it, twisting it this way and that, when all of a sudden, the whole lid released and lifted up with a silent, smooth movement.

He fell backwards onto the sand, forgetting that he wanted it to open. He'd never encountered the materials or mechanisms this box was made off. He needed Godwin. He'd know what to do. Christopher wiped the sweat of his brow, fighting the shakiness in his limbs.

It took all his self-control not to escape and fetch help. He might have done it too, if at that moment the girl in the box hadn't sat up and looked at him, with eyes even bluer than his own. They stared at each other for what felt like an eternity although it was probably only a minute.

Clearing his throat, Christopher croaked, "Hi, I'm Christopher, I'm, well, I found you drifting and pulled you out, then I thought you might be dead, so I tried to open the, whatever it is, and pressed this round thing, which made the glass lift and well, you're not dead. What I mean to say is, I'm glad you're alive. Sorry, maybe I shouldn't have opened the thing." His painful monologue came to an end and he held his breath. Listening to himself, it sounded unbelievable even to him.

What he really wanted to say was, "Who are you and where did you come from?" She inclined her head slightly, her hair appeared to be made up of lots of strands that were light blonde almost silver in color.

"Where am I?" Her voice perplexed him; it had a soft, modulated sound. It didn't fit with any dialect he knew.

"On the east coast of Defenascire."

Her eyes seemed to memorize everything about him, taking in his soft leather shoes, his green tunic and brown trousers.

"What year is it?"

Swallowing at the knot in his throat, he softly said, "One thousand and twenty A.D."

"One thousand years." She exhaled as a tremor ran through her. *It wasn't a dream or a drug.*

She couldn't explain how she got there or how she was able to understand and speak the Old English the man spoke, old-fashioned pronouns and all. It wasn't as if she was connected to her AI. The silence in her head was overwhelming.

"One thousand and twenty if you want to be exact." His voice trailed away as she looked at him with a delicate eyebrow lifted. She took hold of the sides of the box and hopped out, landing in front of him in the sand. Taking in her clothing, an odd feeling took hold of him, as if his eyes were lying to him.

Her clothes were like nothing he'd seen. Her leg coverings almost resembled the chausses he wore, except they were in one piece, fitting snugly around her hips without any tunic over her legs. Her top was white with long sleeves, like an inner tunic, but it wasn't material he'd seen before. The shoes on her feet looked foreign and he stared at the white things without blinking for a moment.

*A thousand years, she couldn't mean…*A light touch to his forearm startled him and he found she had moved closer to him.

"I'm sorry, I've not thanked you."

Christopher shoved his shaky left hand through his hair, "Did not do much. Could not leave you in the box." He took a small step back from her.

She inclined her head again, "If memory serves me right, this is around the end of the dark ages. So, no electricity, Wi-Fi, satellites, or anything remotely technological." She bit her lower lip, revealing a row of white teeth, "El made sure they couldn't find me." How it was possible she couldn't figure out, but the fact that he had helped her even in this unexpected way was—

Her body suddenly seemed to go limp and Christopher sprang forward, catching her beneath her arms. He dragged her away from the water and settled her down. Panic wanted to make him throw up. If only home wasn't so far away.

He stared into the darkness of the cove under the cliff, grabbed hold of the end of the box and pulled it towards the cove. When the rocks got too low for his head, he dropped the end, went round to the other and pushed it in as deep as he could until it was above sea level. For extra safety he packed a few large rocks around it, hoping it would stay hidden. For some unknown reason, he felt the box was important, although it appeared completely empty inside. He heard a noise, and glanced at the girl, who was sitting up again.

Crouching next to her, he asked, "You alright?"

"Yes, thank you. I need some light."

Christopher looked up at the gray, overcast sky, "We do not have a lot of that I am afraid, especially not this time of the year, but if you will come with me, I can find you a warm fire and some food."

Her bright eyes found his, seemingly measuring him. He wanted to look away but couldn't.

She stretched out her hand to him, "My name is Alexa, or Lexi for short."

He took her hand, which was cool to the touch, "I am Christopher."

She kept hold of his hand while she stood up, her head only as high as the middle of his chest.

"I'm not from here, Christopher, as you might have realised. I don't think explaining will help. You'll need to trust me that I mean your world no harm, but in a way, you are protecting me from others who want to destroy me. El sent me to you to keep me safe."

His mouth had gone dry, and he licked over his lips, "I do not understand."

Her hand tightened around his, "It's hard to explain. I'm from another time in the future, where the world looks vastly different. Someone is trying to kill me and El chose to hide me here with you." She looked around the deserted little beach.

Somewhere near his temple, a headache had started to

throb. He couldn't process what she was saying. He pulled his hand out of hers.

"We need to head home, it is getting late." *What will Mother say?* A faint sweat broke out on his forehead.

"Don't worry. It will be all right." Her quiet voice interrupted his thoughts.

She didn't know his mother.

They climbed the steep path to the cliff top, where his mare was grazing a few feet away. She lifted her head and gave a questioning whinny. "Come on, Hilda, time to go." She came obediently when she heard his voice. Alexa stroked Hilda's velvet nose and the horse stood quietly. Christopher helped her up first and then swung up behind her. She was tiny against him and Hilda easily cantered back with them both.

The sky was darkening as they approached the gate. A welcoming fire could be seen inside the open square where a few servants were cooking the evening meal. Christopher steered Hilda around to the back where the stables were, and they dismounted.

He looked down at Alexa, marvelling at how blue her eyes looked even in the semi-darkness. "Listen, we might need to tell my mother that I found you unconscious and you lost your memory, or something."

She took both his hands in hers, "I need to adjust my clothes."

"We have a servant girl your age, but her clothes might not be suitable—" his words got stuck in his throat as before his eyes her clothing seemed to rearrange itself into a dress with long wide sleeves, a thin bodice and a wide skirt. The navy-blue color matched her eyes, with white trims and sleeves. She tied her hair back, throwing the hood of the dress over it. She started humming a soft tune, the sound all at once calming him, like a familiar forgotten lullaby.

"This suits me, right?" She smiled for the first time, the smile of a younger girl.

Christopher swallowed, "Alexa…" the question in his voice chased her smile away.

"Will you trust me?" She bit her lower lip again.

Footsteps sounded behind them and Christopher swung around, hiding her behind him.

"There you are, laddie, I was wondering when you'll be back." The jovial, round face of Stephen, their horse and grounds keeper, greeted him.

"Hilda could do with a good brush down and feed. Thank you, Stephen."

Stephen spotted Alexa behind Christopher and his bushy eyebrows lifted up, "And this? A lassie?"

"Hi, I'm Alexa."

He ignored her greeting and scratched his head. "This is a weird one, laddie, your mother might not be pleased."

"She needs a place to stay for a few nights."

The big man shook his head, "Good luck with that, laddie." He took hold of Hilda's halter and led her away, muttering to himself with his rolling r's.

They started walking around the wooden fort. Christopher's stomach felt knotted as he entered. The interior room was large with an earthen floor, fireplace on the one side and table and chairs on the other. Animal skins lay on the floor as coverings. To the back there were rooms for sleeping quarters.

Deer antlers and the stuffed head of a bear hung against the walls. A fair-haired young man lay on his side near the fire, sipping out of a cup. He looked up as Christopher came in and a smile stole across his face.

"You're back! I told old Tomler off for being so hard on you today. Hope you didn't take it to heart."

Heat flushed across Christopher's face. "Thanks, Godwin."

A cold hand tugged his fingers and he looked down at Alexa who had moved from behind him. "Godwin, this is Alexa. Alexa, this is Godwin."

A low whistle came from Godwin, "Where did you find this beautiful creature?"

She made a low bow, and smiled at him, "Christopher saved my life today."

A look of incredulity flashed across Godwin's face, "Really? What did he do? Chase off a bear, grapple with a snake?"

It was said in jest, but Alexa frowned, "Much more than that, actually, but I'll let him tell it." She looked up at Christopher with an encouraging glance.

Taking a deep breath, he said, "She'd fallen off her horse and lay unconscious by the side of the road. I happened to come across her and revived her with some water. She's had a hard knock on her head and has lost her memory temporarily."

He just lied to Godwin. His gut clenched, but the truth was too strange even to explain to his best friend. He was still reeling from what she'd done with her clothes outside. The headache behind his temple throbbed harder.

He settled Alexa near the fire and fetched them both a drink. A rustle of material made him look up in alarm as a tall woman came into the room. Her dark hair was taken up, leaving her neck bare. There was something regal about her even though their home was not nearly a palace.

"Who's this?" She stared at Alexa, who had gotten up and made a small curtesy.

"I'm Alexa."

They stared at each other, warm bright blue eyes looking into light blue icy ones.

"I'm Lady Audrey."

Christopher moved his hand and the icy stare shifted to him. "Why do you bring strangers to our home, Christopher?"

"I found her next to the road. She was unconscious, she had hit her head. I helped revive her, and what, I couldn't leave her by the road now could I? No respectable man would do that. She just needs to stay for a day or two till we figure out where she's from." He broke away from his mother's stare and looked at the floor, his shoulders slumped.

She looked back at Alexa, her forehead wrinkled slightly, "Well, Alexa, it seems our Christopher had done you a good turn. Maybe you could repay him in some way one day. You are welcome to stay until you remember where you are from."

Her voice had lost none of its iciness, but Alexa smiled at her. "Thank you, my lady, you are too kind and your son too, for saving me today."

"Ghmfff." His mother made a dismissive gesture and sat down next to Godwin. "Please get me a drink, Godwin." Her voice held a note of warmth and she followed the young man as he walked to the table.

Turning back to Alexa she said, "Has Christopher told you that his father is away? He went to meet Canute the Great, our King. We tried to resist his forces, but they were too many for us and took our land by force four years ago. It's a wonder he hasn't come down all the way here and burned our houses to the ground too. You know that though, I presume?"

She took the cup from Godwin, rewarding him with a smile. "I daresay our men will be required to fight in his army and conquer more lands for him.

Alexa sat looking into the fire, seemingly mesmerized by it. Christopher who was nearest to her, was the only one who could hear the gentle hum that emanated from her. Carefully without drawing his mother's attention, he studied Alexa and saw that her hair which was hidden beneath her hood, was... *Glowing, her hair is glowing!* Springing up he placed himself between his mother and Alexa, standing in front of the fire, pretending to warm his hands.

"It was a cold day, today, I'm glad the fire is so hot."

His mother's eyebrows shot up, "Fires are always hot."

Godwin lazily threw in, "The weather has been foul lately, wish spring would hurry up and come properly." His gaze fell on Alexa and his eyes sprang to Christopher, who was now facing away from the fire, pretending to heat his back. Christopher gave him an imperceptible shake of his head.

The door opened, letting the cool night air in. A servant brought in bowls of steaming stew. Christopher handed Alexa hers, her hair had stopped glowing and had become a light brown, similar to his own. He blinked a few times and shook his pounding head. He sat down next to her and ate without tasting the succulent beef and vegetable broth. Godwin feigned disinterest, but Christopher caught him looking at Alexa with a speculative look in his eye.

When they were done, the servant removed the bowls and Lady Audrey gave a yawn, "I'm going to go to sleep, Christopher, give our guest your sleeping quarters, you can sleep in here."

Christopher got up, "Come, I'll show you where to rest."

She followed him to the back, where there were three separate rooms, the smallest of the three contained a soft straw bed.

"Thank you, Christopher." He inclined his head, her voice was different, it contained the dialect of their area, and sounded like a younger version of his mother.

"Sleep well." He turned and fled back to the fireplace. Grabbing an extra log, he stoked the fire before sitting down opposite Godwin.

In a quiet voice, Godwin said, "Out with it, where did you find her, really?"

Christopher pulled at his tunic, clutching his hands tight, before releasing a breath, "You think I'm lying?"

Godwin snorted, "I've known you all my life, there isn't anything you can keep from me."

Christopher's cheeks flushed, and he pulled his head down to stare at the ground. *He doesn't suspect, does he?*

"Come on, out with it. There is something strange about her."

"Okay, but it's going to sound unbelievable." Christopher proceeded to tell him how he had found her in the box up to where she now lay sleeping in his bed. He glanced over to Godwin and saw his face was scowling, his blue eyes dark.

"What were you thinking, Christopher? That girl isn't

natural, she—she might be a witch or a sorcerer or a demon for all we know."

"She's not evil. I'm sure. She said someone is trying to kill her, she's hiding."

Godwin had trouble keeping his voice down, "And you just believe her? Maybe they're hunting her because she is dangerous, and you brought her here!"

"Hush, keep it down. What's up with you? Just because she's different doesn't have to mean she's evil. Can't you trust my instincts?" His hands were moving in jerks as he emphasised his words. He covered his face with his hands, closed his eyes and tried to take a few deep breaths.

Godwin moved until he was next to him and placed his arm around Christopher's shoulders, "I'm sorry, it's just you are more trusting than me, and I feel responsible for protecting you as your older brother. For all that I know, she's placed a spell on you. From what you've told me, I'm not even sure she's human."

His other hand moved to the hilt of his sword. "Maybe we should just play it safe and send her away tomorrow."

Christopher lifted his head and fisted his hands on his lap, "I am not under her spell." He ground out slowly.

Godwin patted him on the shoulder, "Good to know. You are not just my brother but my best friend after all. "

Christopher swallowed, and glanced at him, his body relaxing a fraction, "And you mine." There must have been something in his voice betraying him, because Godwin removed his hand and shifted away from him.

"Let's sleep on it and decide what to do tomorrow." Godwin settled down on the animal skin across from Christopher who followed suit, laying down on one by his feet. The fire was burning low. As he closed his eyes it felt like he kept hearing the clanging of the box against the rocks. Thump, thump. Maybe he should've ignored it.

The familiar sight of Heathrow Airport infused Ruth with a sense of homecoming. Unforeseen tears gathered in her eyes. They'd left at five a.m. from New York and thanks to a five-hour time difference were arriving at five in the afternoon despite only a seven-hour flight. The stress of the past few days threatened to unhinge her. At least it seemed they weren't being pursued. During the flight, James had hacked into the passenger list and no one seemed suspicious. Their fake passports didn't flag any security issues, even the one Alexa got for Langdon worked fine.

Ruth hugged herself, there was a drizzle outside the large glass doors by the exit. They had been debating where to spend the night as the first available flight to China only left the next morning.

"We could stay at my parents." *Where had that come from?*

James's frown deepened. "Do you think they'd mind?"

She shrugged. "They are pretty easy-going." The little fact that she hadn't been to see them in fourteen years was beside the point.

James wiped his hand across his face, his eyes looked red-rimmed, "Fine. Let's get a taxi."

They didn't have any luggage, a fact which irked Ruth the most. They would need to go find a store later that evening. Some grocery stores were open twenty-four hours and usually sported a small selection of clothes. She tried to distract herself by making a list of things she needed in her head.

The taxi made its way slowly through the evening traffic, at times it even stood still. As they passed all the familiar landmarks, Ruth's heart felt ready to break apart. Why had she stayed away so long? The reasons were long and many, but right now they all seemed empty. They entered Kensington, one of London's richest boroughs. There was an estate hidden amongst the mansions, where the state provided housing to the portion of poor middle-class people who couldn't afford their own houses.

This was where Ruth grew up. A poor kid from a rich suburb. The shame she'd become used to as a child rippled through her chest. Last time she'd been here, it was to introduce James, her future husband to her parents. They met her parents in an upper-class restaurant. She would never have taken him to her home. Keeping her head down she avoided looking out at the rows of yellow flats.

The taxi came to a stop and they got out. James paid the fare as Langdon stood watching a few youths kicking a ball on a small square of grass. Ruth knocked at the blue door, number thirteen, but wasn't prepared for it opening straight away and staring into her mother's blue eyes. Her hair lay in gray waves around her face, a face much more wrinkled than Ruth remembered.

"Ruthie?" Her mom softly whispered before pulling her into a hug. For the longest moment Ruth stood rigidly before she melted into her mother's round soft embrace.

"Hi Mum."

"Frank, our baby's home! Ruthie's here!"

She heard rather than saw her father come up behind her mother and felt his fleshy arms surround them both.

"Poppet." She couldn't help but giggle at that old endearment.

Her mom was wiping her own cheeks, her face flushed with a happy smile, "Where's my manners, come in everyone. Come in." She bustled them into the living room, where everything looked much the same as before.

Saggy, dirty white leather couches, check. Brown faded carpet, check. Cheesy flower painting on the wall, check. Ruth was pulled down beside her mom, with her dad easing himself on her other side, while James and Langdon sat down across from them on the other couch.

With her hands held by a parent each, Ruth couldn't help but feel a warmth in her belly. She didn't spare James a look, not wanting to see what he thought of her parents' house. She didn't care what he thought anymore.

"I'm sorry I haven't visited you in such a long time."

"Oh, hush. We know you've been busy. Raising a family overseas and moving so much and all." Her mom smiled at her, "We've enjoyed getting to know Alexa these past years so much, it's such a shame she couldn't come with you." A feeling of unreality crept over Ruth. She'd never told them about Alexa. She could feel James's eyes on her.

He cleared his throat, "When did you last speak to Alexa?"

Her mom looked at her dad with a frown, "Last week, was it Frank? She video-called us to explain she was going on a special course or something, and that you might possibly visit us this time. That's why she sent us that large package to keep for you."

"You've done such a good job of raising that child. She's a joy to us, even from afar." Her father gruffly offered.

Questions swamped Ruth's mind, but she couldn't voice

them without revealing that she had no idea Alexa had been in contact with them.

Her father was still looking at her, so she blurted out, "Thank you, Dad. She is an easy child. Much easier than I was."

"I wouldn't say that, you were and always will be our darling daughter, Ruthie." Her mother countered with her head inclined.

"So, who is this young man, then? Alexa's boyfriend?" Ruth's dad voiced looking directly at Langdon.

Langdon started and shook his head, although his cheeks flushed. James eyed him curiously. The thought had never crossed his mind that a young man might like his daughter. His daughter. He let those two words sink deeper into him.

"I'm just a friend." Langdon responded at last.

"Yes, he's travelling with us to visit a colleague of his father's in China." James covered for him.

"Do you want to stay overnight with us? We can make beds in the living room for the men, and Ruth, your old room is still yours."

"Yes, thank you, Mum. That would be great. Our flight leaves at nine tomorrow morning."

"Frank, why don't you and the men go get some takeaways in the high street for tonight." Doreen hustled the men out. Ruth wandered down the short hall to her old bedroom on the left. It was only a two-bedroom flat. The bathroom was across from her room and her parents' room was situated at the end of the hallway. The faded wallpaper with its lines of daisies still graced the walls. She remembered them gluing it on for her sixth birthday. Her bed was stacked full of her teddies. On the bed rested a large box. She sank down on the bed next to it.

"You going to open it?"

Her mom appeared with a mug of tea in each hand. "I've been very curious about it." She grinned mischievously making Ruth smile.

In no time the box was open, and Ruth took in what looked like hand luggage. Soft pyjamas, toothbrush and paste, her favourite comfortable jeans and a cobalt blue pretty shirt all lay neatly packed. Ruth's eyes threatened to tear up again at the thoughtfulness of her daughter.

There was a box of biscotti biscuits she liked, which she promptly opened and offered to her mum. They dunked the biscuits and sat on the bed with the half-unpacked box between them. It felt like a mini Christmas. There were two sets of clean clothes and a comfortable cotton jumper. Ruth pulled out the envelope underneath the clothes but placed it aside for later.

"I expected something special." Her mom's face was quizzical. "How did Alexa know you'd lose your luggage?"

Ruth shrugged, "She's good at anticipating things." She paused and softly said, "I miss her."

"I've missed you." Her mom stated, staring into her teacup. Ruth reached out her hand, one younger version holding an older version, "I'm sorry, Mum."

"Me too."

Ruth inhaled, "As soon as Alexa is back, we'll plan a long holiday together. Maybe Portugal? You've always wanted to go to Portugal, haven't you?"

Doreen smiled through her tears, "I'd be happy anywhere as long as I'm with you and my beautiful granddaughter."

Sean strode into their New York base of operations looking like a thunder cloud.

Mole squinted at him and said, "I take it you didn't find her?"

"No! She's vanished into thin air." Sean struggled to keep his voice down. He sat down behind his desk. Bringing up all the files he had on James and Ruth and everyone they knew at college; he went through it again. The past few days had been fruitless.

Back in Berkley, he found out who had rented the apartment. Langdon White and his sister. They'd paid the rent in advance for six months. What kind of young man had that much in savings? He could find very little about him. His work was listed as self-employed.

Sean grunted in frustration. He didn't even know what Alexa was doing there. Why did she go to the professor? Who was Langdon? A young man's jacket and skateboard was in the lab but according to the internet, the professor's son died seven years ago. Maybe Langdon was a student of the professor's or a lab assistant?

He looked up, "Mole, place a watch on our frequency monitors in the airport. If we have a ping for the perfect frequency Alexa radiates, I want to know immediately!"

Mole typed for a few minutes. "Done. What else?"

Sean looked at his screen. There was another professor, but he was on the other side of the world. Maybe he could phone him.

"Get me the number for Professor Li Geming."

It must have been midnight, but Ruth still tossed and turned in her bed. She heard her bedroom door open and saw James' profile against the hall-way light as he slipped in. He shut the door behind him softly, leaving the room semi-dark except for the faint light coming from the streetlamp outside her window. He came over and slid down to the ground, with his back resting against her bed. She studied his side profile, noticing the strong, handsome jawline she'd always found so attractive.

"You can't sleep either?" She said to break the silence.

"No." He was quiet, had been quiet the whole evening. It wasn't like him.

"I'm sorry." His words came out haltingly.

"For what?"

"Everything." This was so unlike James that Ruth sat up, hugging her knees to herself. She didn't know how to respond.

"Your parents are nice, honest people." James stopped.

Ruth's nails bit into her palms, "Yeah, they are. They deserved a better life." After a moment she went on in a subdued tone, "My dad hurt his back when he was younger, which meant he couldn't be a plumber anymore. He tried various odd jobs through the years, but the back always did him in. Mum never studied for anything and worked in a grocery store all her life. They scraped together every penny to send me to university when I got the grant."

"Unlike us lucky rich kids, who had it fall into our laps, right?" Ruth kept quiet. "This was why you joined the Salem group, wasn't it? To bring equality. No more a few privileged rich, but a fairer distribution of funds, so everyone can have a decent house with a garden." His voice tapered away.

Ruth rubbed one hand over the other thinking back to the past. "I always dreamed of having a garden with a dog. I had a friend in school who lived in one of the mansions. I visited her once and she had everything a girl could dream of. I was too ashamed to invite her to my house. Later in high school she was one of the cool, rich kid groupies and we council kids were snubbed by them. We couldn't afford the latest phones and accessories they had." Ruth was dismayed at how bitter her voice sounded even after so many years.

James cleared his throat, "As one of the cool, rich kids I can only apologize. If it's any consolation, those gadgets were a poor substitute for loving, present parents. If I had had a choice between growing up with your type of parents and my type of parents, who I barely saw, I think yours win. It's no wonder you are such a great mother. Sometimes I watch you with Alexa and I feel like an outsider. I don't know how to connect emotionally or relationally with you both, even though I want to."

Ruth touched her throat. James never opened up about his feelings. Absentmindedly she traced a circle on her duvet, "I've always admired you. You're so good at doing stuff, while I get all emotional."

James turned his head towards her, "There is nothing wrong with emotions. I stuff them down, which isn't healthy. No wonder you don't know how I feel about you." He turned over onto his knees, kneeling by her bed, leaning on his elbows.

"Do you know that the first time I saw you come into Professor Li Geming's class; I fell in love with you? You were so vivacious. Curves in all the right places, a smile bright enough to light the room and a softness in your eyes that melted right through the frost in mine. But I couldn't let you see that. I couldn't let you see me. My upbringing convinced me that I wasn't worth loving. There was no chance on earth that you could love someone like me."

Her breath hitched, her heart was racing and there was a fluttery feeling in her belly. She wished she could see his face more clearly; his eyes were dark in the semi-light. She reached out for his hand, and he took it, holding it tightly in his.

"I haven't treated you the way I wanted to treat my wife one day. I kept thinking one day, when Salem was established. One day, when we have time, and now we are being hunted and Salem is hanging in the balance and I find myself regretting every single choice I've made since I met you."

"Do you regret marrying me, and having Alexa?" Her voice came haltingly.

"No! But I regret not going about it in the right way. Using the cause as an excuse, believing that you only married me for it. I regret using our daughter for the project although she is amazing. What if she dies because of this? Alexa said none of the outcomes worked out well. None, Ruth! Why didn't she tell us sooner?"

"Would you have believed her?"

He groaned, "I don't know. We have the most advanced AI at our fingertips, and we didn't use it to work out whether our vision was feasible. How stupid is that?"

"I know." She pressed his hand.

"Alexa says that Professor Li Geming manipulated us into forming the Salem group. That he basically brainwashed us."

"You don't think so?"

"I don't know. The more I think about it, the more I realise how many of my ideals I get from him. I never questioned it that much. I—I look up to him." He pushed his fist against his mouth.

"He does make a convincing argument. Who can argue that a world of equality and peace isn't a worthy cause to devote our lives to?" A shiver ran through her. "We chose it. He might have baited us, but we bought it; hook, line and sinker." She let go of James' hand and hugged herself again.

He looked at her, "Do you think we might have been misled somehow?"

"All I know is that instead of being happy, I'm miserable." She hesitated, "Do you know that she can't even enjoy a movie? Within five minutes she knows the outcome, but she still watches it with me, just to keep me company." Ruth lay down again, in a fetal position.

He sat next to her bed until he heard her breathing even out. Memories of watching her sleep in the past stole over him. Time to leave.

CHAPTER

6

Christopher awoke with a start; the birds were chirping, and the morning light had started warming up the ground outside. The fire was out, and the cold had crept into his bones. He stretched, there was a rustling and Alexa came into the room. Her dress looked perfect, no wrinkles or sign of having slept in it. She came towards him without a smile.

"Morning, Christopher."

"Morning, Alexa. Did you sleep well?"

She hesitated, "It was fine, thank you. I heard you tell your friend about me."

"Yes, he can help us." He looked towards the door his face pinched. *Brother or friend, what does it matter.*

"I'm afraid he's going to disappoint you."

"What do you mean?"

She hesitated. "I sense fear in him."

Christopher scoffed, "Afraid? Godwin? He's braver than two of me."

"No. You are braver than you think, but you might need to be very brave if you mean to keep me safe."

"Well, you are up early." Lady Audrey came into the room from outside, glancing at them with suspicion.

Alexa curtsied, "Thank you for allowing me to stay, Lady Audrey. It might be best if I leave today."

"Have you remembered where you come from?"

"No, but I'm sure I will if I return to where I got hurt."

"Hmm. Funny thing is, there is no sign of you getting hurt, no swelling on your head." Her ice-cold eyes stared at Alexa with hostility. "And a little birdie told me that you are not all that you seem."

"Leave her alone, Mother. I found her, and I'm responsible for her." Christopher's cheeks were flushed, and his eyes sparked. *She was right.*

"Bah, responsible? Since when have you ever been able to be responsible for anything? Stephen!"

"Yes, my lady?" His big bulk filled the doorway.

"I want you to secure this — this girl in the empty stable, until our master comes back and deals with her."

"Yes, my lady."

Christopher's body was trembling, his breathing fast, but he knew he stood no chance against Stephen.

"You're making a mistake!" He got out between clenched teeth, only to hear his mother's mocking jeer.

"Really? Since when do you have an opinion? Get out; out of my sight. Your father can deal with you too, when he comes back."

Alexa didn't protest when Stephen took her by the arm. After they left, the tension in the air crackled between Christopher and his mother.

Godwin came in, looked at them both and said, "I think I'll go hunting today. Want to join me, Christopher?" He turned around and Christopher found himself following him. Better Godwin than his mother.

They had barely ridden out the gate before he said, "Why did you tell her?"

Godwin shrugged, "I had to. She isn't safe."

"You don't even know her! How can you just judge by outer appearance?"

"Since when do you care so much about a total strange waif who arrives on your doorstep? I would have thought you'd have better sense and trust your friend and mother."

Christopher was silent for a few moments, before pulling in his horse, "Do you know what the problem is? You both think I'm useless. You don't trust my judgment and I'm telling you she's not dangerous. Why won't you listen to me?"

Godwin pulled in his horse too, and turned towards Christopher, "What's gotten into you? I think she has bewitched you."

"She's not a witch."

"Oh, so what is she?"

"I don't know, but I won't let you destroy her just because you are afraid."

Thunder stole across Godwin's face, "I'm not afraid of her."

Christopher looked, really looked at his friend and for the first time saw something of his mother and father in him. Something predatory.

A coldness invaded him, and he wiped a stray tear off his cheek, "I'm not going with you." Pulling Hilda around, he kicked her in the sides and galloped away.

They hadn't gone far, so he arrived back at the stables within a few minutes.

Stephen came towards him, with eyebrows raised, "And now what, laddie?"

"I forgot something. Leave Hilda saddled, I'm in a hurry." He went into their home, via the back door, listening for his mother's voice. He could hear her scold the servants in the front room, and silently stole into his room. He moved a stone away to open his secret stash, and filled a velvet pouch with all the coins he had.

Outside again, he took one piece of cold cured ham from the storehouse and attached it to his saddle along with a water pouch. To his relief, Stephen was busy getting water from the well at the opposite corner from the stables. He stole into the stables to the empty one at the end, expecting to find Alexa tied up, but she was standing in the stall, with broken cords on the hay, quietly waiting, as if she knew he would come. Her dress had altered into a green tunic, matching his own attire.

He helped her up onto Hilda, expecting someone to sound the alarm at any moment. She sat in front of him like last time, with a cloak covering her head. He urged Hilda on, and they galloped for the gate. No one sounded an alarm or even gave them any notice. It was as if he was invisible to them.

They rode for two hours due north. It was his stomach that alerted him that it was lunch time and he pulled Hilda off the path into the woods. They found a secluded area and dismounted. He broke off a piece of meat for her. She smiled her thanks and sat down cross-legged to eat it.

Christopher followed suit. He was staring at her without realizing it.

She smiled, that youthful smile that didn't fit with her adult voice and manners, "What are you thinking?"

He swallowed and then asked what he could no longer not ask, "What are you?"

She crouched down, grabbed a stick and started drawing in the ground. He crouched down opposite her, studying her intensely. What if she was a witch?

"I'm not a witch."

He started, "How did you?"

She shrugged. "I, it's hard to explain. I'm not from your world in this time, remember? I'm from the future."

"Future, you mean ahead of our time. But it's not possible."

"Who decides what is possible and what is not possible?"

I think I'm losing my mind.

"I know it's hard to imagine, but you aren't going crazy."

"Stop doing that! It's like you're hearing my thoughts!"

Alexa lifted her head, dipping it sideways, "I can hear horses approaching, from the direction we came. I think Godwin is with them."

"What was I thinking? I could never outrun Godwin. I'm no match for him."

"But you aren't alone, are you?" Alexa looked at him with her eyes brighter than before. She held her hand out to him and he took it. Humming the strange tune she hummed the last time, he let it flow through him, calming him. Even Hilda stepped up to them and held her head near Alexa as if she listened to the tune too. From afar, Christopher could hear the horses approach and pass them without stopping. *Godwin.*

"You love him, don't you?"

He pulled his hand out of hers, shaking his head, "He's my brother. He is, or was, my best friend too."

She kept looking at him and he frowned, "I can't."

"But you do."

"He's everything I'd like to be."

"I understand."

Christopher absently stroked Hilda's neck. "I'm supposed to be a man. Be like Godwin. Instead, I'm soft, careful, with a head fuller of dreams than anything useful. I hate fighting and hunting and everything a man is supposed to be so good at."

Alexa didn't reply. She was looking in the direction the group with Godwin had gone. "I think we should head back to the coast."

"Find the box?"

"Maybe." She shrugged, looking up at the clouds through which a smattering of sunshine could be seen. Throwing off her hood and closing her eyes, she seemed to drink it in. Hesitantly he reached out and touched a strand of her hair. It felt smooth. Everything about her seemed alive.

"It feels strange to be disconnected." She quietly said, her eyes still closed. "I can't see ahead."

"If you could see ahead before, did you see this?"

She looked at him with a small grin, "Actually no. I did not see this as a possibility."

He shrugged, "Then someone bigger than you saw it."

Inclining her head, she gazed at him making him squirm.

"What?"

Nothing."

He mounted Hilda and held out his hand for her. "Let's go."

Seth Hudson went over the footage for the hundredth time. It made no sense. The group of men carried the covered box into the containment room. The camera inside the room showed them depositing it onto the table, leaving and locking the door. Their progress out was recorded by all the other cameras on the grounds. They left with an empty van, that was for sure. Then came the part which blew his mind. In the locked room, it looked like the box suddenly melted under the ridiculous cloth they'd covered it with, leaving the navy thing draped over the table.

No box. No girl. And the men who kidnapped her also seemed to have vanished into thin air. He couldn't get a hold of them anywhere. What was going on? He resisted the panic wanting to surge up in him. It was time to activate the other part of Plan B. He unlocked the safe hidden in his office and took out a special phone, dialling a number.

As soon as the person on the other end answered, he said, "Tell FL the girl has vanished. See if he can find her."

He listened for a moment. "You can deal with them when they reach you. Keep them alive for now. They might give us leverage with the girl."

The man on the other end said something else.

Seth gave a gruff chuckle, "When have I ever let you down, my old friend? I'm tying up all the loose ends on this side. We should be able to activate our plan on schedule. I was hoping to avoid the direct force, but we have no other option now. I have a team ready to attack. On the morning of the twelfth of April, FL can attack the NY stock exchange just as planned and on the same day we'll steal their keys."

He sniggered as the other man responded. "That you can say again. It will be a Resurrection Sunday the world won't soon forget. The resurrection of a new world order. Of peace. For Salem."

The other man echoed his sentiments and they hung up. Seth Hudson secured the phone before sitting down at his desk. He couldn't resist the urge to watch the footage again. That vanishing box made him uneasy. There were factors at play that he couldn't control; that he didn't understand. He didn't like it. Not one bit.

They stopped to rest twice, but still the four-hour trek to the coast was tiresome. The sun was nearer to the horizon, hovering over the water when they reached the spot. Christopher was relieved to find the box just where they left it. Alexa stood facing the water, humming under her breath. Christopher had pulled the box nearer to the waterline and went to stand next to her.

The wind picked up and blew their hair back. Alexa placed her hand on the side of the box and with the other took Christopher's hand. A noise overhead made him turn his head. There was the sound of pebbles rolling, and down the small path Godwin came striding down. He had his sword in his hand, his face set in a fierce frown.

Christopher turned to face him, keeping Alexa and the box shielded behind him.

"Haven't you done enough damage for one day, Christopher?" Godwin demanded, wiping across his brow. He looked tired and dirty after riding the whole day. "I'm tired of this. Get out of the way, so we can deal with this witch."

"No." Too soft. "NO." He said in a louder voice, pulling back his shoulders and lifting his chin.

"Come on, we both know who would win a fight between us. There's no use for this charade."

"So you're just going to kill me?"

Godwin's eyes and mouth opened wide. "Don't be ridiculous. You're my best friend, my brother!"

"Then you'd give me some credibility. Alexa is under my protection."

Godwin's eyebrows pinched together, "But I'm trying to protect you. She's a stranger. Why do you care so much about her?"

"I don't know. Maybe because she is a human being, and all human beings deserve to be treated with respect."

The wind that had been gently blowing around them seemed to increase. It whipped at their hair and clothes with more strength.

Godwin rubbed his eyes because all of a sudden Christopher didn't seem so solid anymore. He ran forward, but just as he reached out his hand, they vanished before his eyes. It felt as if the wind had simply picked them up and made them disappear. The only thing left was their footprints in the sand. Godwin stared around frantically, hearing the men he had left up the cliff shout his name. How was he going to explain this? Better to say that he was mistaken, they weren't there. Pretend to keep on searching.

Fierce anger burned through him at the thought that Alexa had taken Christopher from him. If only he'd listened to him more, maybe he could have at least been with him wherever she took him.

It did prove one thing. She was a witch.

Christopher blinked and then blinked again, because the room he was in seemed unreal. He felt a hand in his, and realised Alexa was standing next to him. There was a silver-looking table on which the box rested. All around them were white solid sides.

"Christopher."

His frantic gaze landed on her bright eyes, "Alexa?

Where are we?" He fingered his lips, his eyes large. He was speaking a different language, yet he understood it.

She pressed his hand tighter, "We are back in my time, one thousand years in the future from yours. It seems you translocated back with me."

"Your time?" His head was reeling.

"He told me that you have a role to play in all of this."

"The one you said brought you to me to keep you safe?"

"Yes, El."

"El?"

"El is the One who controls all the power systems of the universe and beyond. He's the one who brought me to you. That someone you thought saw ahead where I couldn't."

Christopher shoved a trembling hand through his hair, "I'm not sure I understand. What language is this?"

Alexa looked around at the door at the other end, "English. We need to get out of here. This is the house of my enemy."

"Enemy!" His voice had gone high. "You've got the wrong man with you as protector."

She smiled at him, "You are here for a different, even more important reason. Stay with me." She walked over to the door and touched the handle. There was a sound of beeping, before the door clicked open. Before his eyes, her clothes reshaped back into the weird stuff she had worn when he first met her.

"They're called sneakers, jeans and a T-shirt." She whispered to him, as they left the room. The house was dark, it was clearly night-time. Alexa stood with her eyes shut for a minute before turning left. Christopher followed her as quietly as he could. If allowed, he would have exclaimed in wonder at all the strange things he saw in this building. They went through a few doors, until they came to one that had vehicles in it.

Christopher recognized what they were through the fact that they had wheels, but he couldn't comprehend how they worked. The low blue one at the far end beeped and Alexa indicated he should get in. He copied the way she lifted the latch and slid in next to her.

"This car has five hundred and fifty horsepower."

"What?"

"It means its engine is as strong as five hundred and fifty horses."

He could only shake his head in bewilderment and stifle his scream as a deep noise started up in front of him and the thing started moving backwards through a garage door that had silently opened behind them. The steering wheel turned by itself. Alexa had activated self-drive and her AI was directing the vehicle to the nearest airport, which was San Jose airport. She erased the video footage in the house, so that no one would know they were there.

Instead of booking flights directly to China, she booked them to London. She generated a passport for Christopher and one for herself to be dropped in a safety deposit box near the airport. Alexa took a photo for the passport via looking at him which could be uploaded straight through her own neuro-processors.

She glanced over to her passenger, who was clutching the seats as if he was going to tumble out of the car at any moment.

"You're going to see a lot in the coming few days you'd never thought possible. Mankind has advanced quite a bit in a thousand years."

"A bit, you say?" He croaked out. "I'm moving, inside a box on wheels, faster than anyone I know has ever gone. Everything is made of materials I don't even recognise. I'm speaking a language I've never learned or heard but suddenly can understand. I might as well have gone to another world."

"Yes, I guess in a way, but most of the changes are superficial. People at their heart are still the same, they just live differently."

He gave her an inquisitive look, "Something gives me the idea that you are not one of the normal people in this world."

She kept quiet. "No. I've been altered. There are things inside me that connect me to the technology in this world, specifically to a very advanced thinking machine, which we call a computer. Technology is the word we use for everything to do with computers and communication. We have a way of communicating called the Web. It's all around the world, and you can communicate and send information over it in seconds. These things I have in me give me the ability to enhance my physical abilities as well as adjust my attire."

"That went straight over my head." He tugged at his ear.

Alexa laughed. "Luckily for you, we aren't measured by our knowledge but by our hearts. You have a good heart, Christopher."

He shook his head, "I'm not sure about that, but if you say so." He took a long look at the dashboard, his eyes roaming over the electronic display, before looking at Alexa, "I hope your El knows what He's doing, but I trust you Alexa." He blew out his cheeks and released them, "Probably because I can sense you have good intentions too."

She placed her hand on her heart, her eyes soft, "We

should try to rest; it's going to be a long journey to get where we're going."

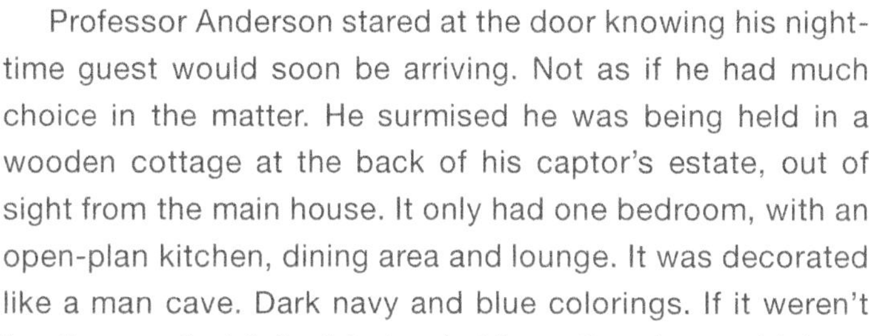

Professor Anderson stared at the door knowing his night-time guest would soon be arriving. Not as if he had much choice in the matter. He surmised he was being held in a wooden cottage at the back of his captor's estate, out of sight from the main house. It only had one bedroom, with an open-plan kitchen, dining area and lounge. It was decorated like a man cave. Dark navy and blue colorings. If it weren't for the small detail of being held captive, he could have imagined himself on holiday.

For reasons he couldn't work out, his captor liked to spend an hour with him in the evenings. They ate together and then played a game of chess. Or two, depending if he won. The man liked to win.

He made no effort to disguise who he was. The professor had met him years ago once or twice, in the company of Professor Li Geming. When Adam's wife died, they offered him a large sum of money, enough to support a lifetime of research and take care of Langdon. He got the message loud and clear. Either he signed over the rights to the nanobots design or something might befall Langdon too. There was no evidence that they orchestrated his wife's death, but he knew.

After he left the group, he had kept a discreet eye on Seth Hudson's career as he was sure the man had done with him. Tonight, right on schedule Seth appeared, a kitchen helper carrying their food behind him. During the meal, Adam observed that Seth wasn't keeping eye contact, his gaze kept bouncing from place to place and he fidgeted.

Finally, Adam said, "Is something wrong?" He clamped his teeth shut and took a deep breath.

Seth stirred, before stabbing another piece of chicken and placing it in his mouth. After chewing, he said, "I might as well tell you. I kidnapped Alexa, but she vanished into thin air." He explained how she had been in the specially designed box, which was sealed, but how it vanished only to reappear again except no Alexa.

"There are a few minutes of video footage missing from my surveillance. Can your nanobots do something like that? Make her appear invisible? Vanish the box?"

Professor Anderson took off his glasses and polished them, "I don't think so. Honestly, I was amazed at what she could do in the few minutes I saw her. I never envisioned any of it could be possible." A bitter smile flashed across his face before he pressed his lips tight.

"The video footage I understand. If she were reconnected with her AI side, she could do anything. But not from within the box."

"Except you never saw her in the box?" He raised his eyebrows, offering the man a questioning gaze.

Seth hit the table with his fisted hand, "It doesn't make any sense. I know they captured her, I know they placed her in the box and delivered her to me. How is she not here!"

Professor Anderson hid his smile and pushed out his chest. He knew that Alexa was the only hope he had of being rescued. The air hung quietly between them.

Bluntly he asked, "Why did you not take me out years ago?" He placed his glasses back on.

Seth lowered his chin, his jaw hard, "We got what we wanted, your rights and silence about the nanobots.

Besides, you are the best nano scientist besides Professor Geming in the world. I needed someone like you in case something happened to Prof Geming." He narrowed his eyes, "I kept tabs on you but knew you would have to be silenced if our plan came into motion and you put two and two together." This he stated in the same calm voice as if he was commenting on the weather.

Adam's nostrils flared, his breathing noisy, "Why are you so heartless? Don't you care about people at all?"

Seth gave a snort of dismissive laughter, "That is where you have it wrong. I care about people a great deal. But I don't want to help only one person, I want to help the whole world."

He leaned forward his one hand on his knee, his eyes intent on Adam, "In order to do that, a few people need to be sacrificed for the greater good. If they knew what they were giving their lives for, they would been willing." Adam's lips compressed tightly; he hid his shaking hands under the table.

"Wouldn't you give your life in exchange for your son to live in a world free of wars, abuse, poverty and corruption? A world of peace? Salem will bring peace. It is the only way to save people from themselves. We are our own worst enemy. We need an unbiased leader that will govern us without any influences of greed, racism or malice." As he spoke his eyes sparkled, his speech becoming more and more animated.

Professor Anderson folded his arms over his stomach, "You honestly believe by having Alexa govern the world, you can create equality and peace?"

A short bark escaped Seth, he jutted out his chin, "No, unfortunately Alexa has proven a failed experiment." His smile was hard and his hand waved in dismissal. "But I have another one who grew up much less exposed to the follies of mankind. He will prove to be a stricter, better ruler."

Adam's eyes widened and he leaned forward, his body tense, "There is another one?"

Seth's brows pinched and he sat back, "I hadn't meant to tell you of him."

He paused; his lips pursed. "Well, I guess you aren't going anywhere."

He pressed a bell, and a servant came to take their plates away, leaving the chess board on the table between them. Seth started setting it up.

"He's actually Professor Li Geming's son. Li Feng is much more disciplined than Alexa. We corrected some mistakes we made with her. He is an improved version and his AI is growing very aggressively. Showing complete independence and alliance with the goals of the Salem Group." He watched Adam waiting to see his reaction, a smug smile playing on his face.

He moved a chess piece. "Your turn."

"Do James and Ruth know about him?" Professor Anderson's forehead was sweating and he felt extremely thirsty. He licked his lips and made his move.

"No. We thought the fewer knew the better. Soon everybody who knew about the Salem group will be no more, anyhow." Seth made another move on the chess board.

Adam felt like throwing up. He moved a bishop without thinking, his thoughts churning. *Another one!*

"By the way, there is a young man travelling with James and Ruth whom I can't help but think must be your son. They are on their way to China to meet with Professor Geming. He has a different alias, which I think Alexa organised for him. It says online that he died a few years ago, but I'm sure that's a lie. It must be him. Curly blond hair, green eyes?" His head tilted, his jaw set.

It took everything for Professor Anderson not to show recognition. "My son did die." He was sweating profusely.

Seth Hudson stared hard at him. "Never mind. We'll soon get his real name out of him and maybe the whereabouts of Alexa. I'm sure she is aware of where they are and probably following them. Checkmate!"

Professor Anderson felt like attacking the man in front of him, but he knew he couldn't make a dent in him. All he could do was grind his teeth and stare with blazing hatred at his retreating back when he left. Would Alexa be able to outsmart Prof. Geming's protégée?

CHAPTER 7

Christopher woke up groggy from the anti-nausea pill Alexa had given him. She gave him herbs to help him relax too. It was a wonder he hadn't freaked out completely when she told him they were going to fly in this monstrosity of a....machine? Was that what they called it? All these contraptions were machines. Releasing a pent-up breath, he leaned back, trying to get his cramped legs into a more comfortable position.

He looked across at Alexa and had to blink repeatedly. He'd forgotten that she had altered her appearance before they checked in for the flight. Her hair was brown, eye color brown, with freckles dotted all over her face. He'd been dazed to see his own face in the little strange book she gave him.

His brain had gone into overload after seeing the flying machines. He wondered what his family would think of him now. If it didn't take a brave man to face all this strangeness, he didn't know what did.

The man across the aisle coughed and Christopher stood up, carefully stepping over Alexa's feet. Her eyes were closed, it appeared as if she was dozing. It felt freeing to stretch out his full length and walk down the narrow path

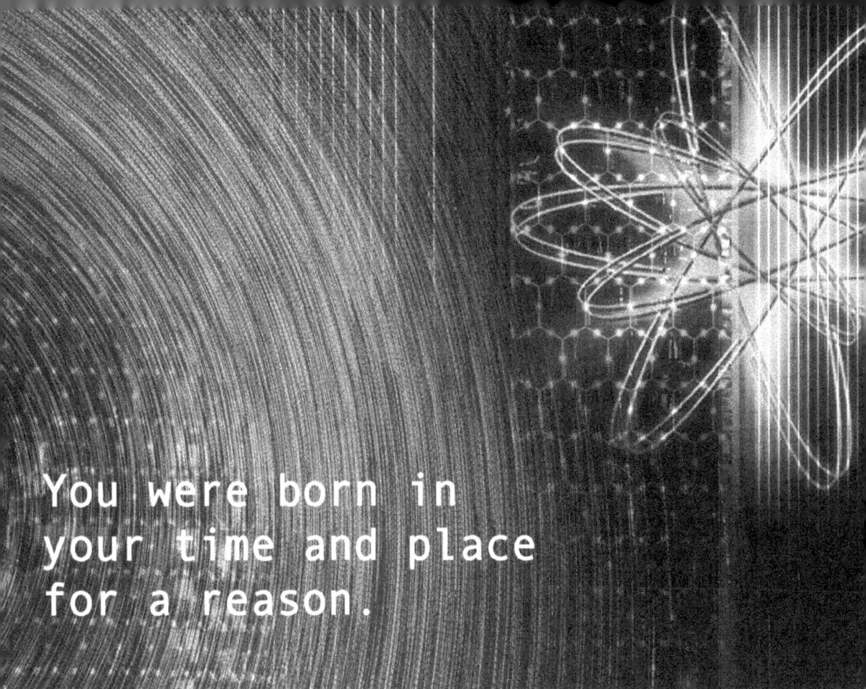

between the seats.

So many people in such a small space. They fascinated him. A young red-haired woman made eye contact and smiled, he smiled back forcing himself to relax. It felt like he stuck out as a stranger from another world, but the first thing Alexa did was to get him similar outfits as herself. He sported jeans, and a blue polo-shirt along with the funny, but comfortable sneakers she wore. Still, he felt alien.

They would soon be landing in what Alexa told him was the place he knew as Londinium. It struck him as hilarious that his father was there at the same time as him, except for the minor detail of a thousand years' time difference. He swallowed at the knot in his throat.

It baffled him how he came to be here. Somehow it had to be God, but he didn't even follow Him. He classed him in the same boat as his parents who were religious. He was of no use to them or to God. So why was all this happening to him? His hands had curled into fists and he forced them to relax. He made his way back to his place beside the small window.

The seatbelt light blinked and a voice over the speakers asked them to take their seats right after he sat down. The machine slanted sideways dipping into a turn. He ventured a look out through the glass and felt his jaw go slack. It was the largest amount of buildings he had ever seen. The river glistened like a blue snake, curving through the city. Who would have thought Londinium would become this massive, sprawling place? There must be an uncountable amount of people living here.

"Beautiful, isn't it?" Alexa leaned past him and looked out.

"Never seen anything like it." Christopher's cheeks flushed. "What's new."

"Hey. You were born in your time and place for a reason. It's not inferior."

"Well, you guys seem to have a better deal. I mean—"

She dipped her chin, tipping her head sideways, "—on appearance yes. Very advanced. But I have my doubts on other aspects. Every era has its own strengths and weaknesses."

"Joys and sorrows." Christopher looked down at the city anew, wondering what all the people living there felt and did. The burning question within him however was why a God he didn't know had brought him here. Why him?

Sean tried to fit his long legs into the space between the seat in front of him and his chair. He hated flying. The moment they got the ping for Alexa's frequency he'd booked himself a flight, following her itinerary. Lucky for him she booked in as Emmeline White. The same name as Langdon White's sister. The flight was heading to London. He had the address for Ruth's parents; Mr and Mrs Clarke who lived in Kensington, committed to memory. It made sense for Alexa to contact her grandparents.

He rubbed his face with both hands, before leaning back. It might be a wild goose chase. Carrie might die all alone in that hospital bed. It was ripping his heart in two to leave her there. He stopped by on his way to the airport. She wasn't looking weaker or stronger. Just the same. At least she opened her eyes for a few moments and smiled at him. He clenched his fists. Life wasn't fair. She didn't do anything to deserve to die like this.

"Why haven't you found her yet?" Professor Li Geming shook his fist in the face of the tall boy with the neat black hair parted on the side standing upright in front of him. The boy's face remained impassive, except for a small tic near his right eye.

"I will soon."

"So you keep saying. Is she better than you?" The professor taunted.

"No." The boy's dark eyes glittered dangerously.

Professor Li turned his back on him, "I'll speak to you again when you've found her." He left the cube-shaped room. The room's one wall was a giant screen. The boy sat down on the lone seat in the middle, facing it.

His dark eyes stared intently at the screen. "One day he won't tell me what to do." His mouth curved upwards on one side. "No. One day no one will tell me what to do. They will all listen to me."

He should thank the girl for running away. She opened the way for him. He would make sure her death was as painless as possible. He perked up as he heard the professor talk on his mobile in his office down the hallway, "He's working on it. Shouldn't take him much longer. They are arriving this morning. I'm meeting them for dinner. I'll let you know what they know."

Li Feng's smile widened. The plot was thickening. Not too many days before they could cripple the world and bring in the new world order. He could hardly wait.

The door opened abruptly, and the tousled blond-haired guy stared at them in confusion. Then he squinted and said, "Alexa?"

"Langdon? What are you doing here?" He pulled them into the house and shut the door behind them, ushering them into the living room, before quickly going to the windows and pulling the curtains shut. The three young people faced each other in the darkened room.

"Boy, am I glad to see you." Langdon grinned, pushing his fringe away. "Who's this?" He looked at Christopher.

"This is Christopher. He is a friend from another place."

"Pleased to meet you." Langdon held out his hand, and Christopher looked at it with raised eyebrows, before touching it quickly.

"You too."

Langdon tilted his head, "You don't shake hands?"

"He's from England, but a thousand years ago." Alexa was watching Langdon's face.

He looked back at her, raising an eyebrow. "Okay. Just when I thought things couldn't get any weirder."

Alexa looked around, "Where's my Grandpa and Grandma?"

"They've gone to buy groceries. Should be back soon."

"Did my parents go to China without you?"

"Yes. I had this strange feeling that I needed to stay behind. Wait for you."

Alexa's hair adjusted to blonde as he spoke and her eyes took on their luminous blue color. She took a step closer to Langdon, reaching for his hand. "I'm glad you did."

He ducked his head, giving her a half smile. "Me too." They looked into each other's eyes for a fraction longer, until Christopher cleared his throat.

"Sorry, but I have no idea what I'm doing here. If there is a plan, I'd like to know it." He flopped down onto the couch, dropping the sports bag he'd been carrying.

Alexa went to sit on the single couch and Langdon sat down next to Christopher. She brought Langdon up to speed with what had been happening to them and he told them his part, including an explanation about his father's abduction to Christopher.

"I'm sorry I haven't found him yet." Alexa quietly told Langdon.

"Hey. You did your best. I still can't believe you went back in time and brought Christopher here with you."

"I can scarcely believe it myself." Mumbled Christopher, who had shut his eyes and laid back his head.

There was a noise at the door and her grandparents came in. They had eyes only for Alexa and dropped their groceries right on the floor.

"Our baby." Frank placed his large, rough hand on her shoulder.

"You're even more beautiful in real life." Doreen gushed before they both hugged her tight.

Alexa wiped at the tears on her cheeks, there was a fluttery feeling in her belly.

"I'm so happy to be here."

"How long are you staying?" Doreen asked with her eyebrows raised, holding her breath.

Alexa was about to answer when she got goose bumps, "Two days."

Christopher and Langdon looked at her back with question marks on their face. More resolutely she stated again, "Two days. We need to stay two days."

"You can stay as long as you want, precious granddaughter." Doreen chortled, it felt good to say it aloud.

"We are going to go to China, to meet up with Mom and Dad, but I want to see the city my mom grew up in and spend time with you." She looked down.

"Are you hungry? What am I saying, teenagers are always hungry. Come help me poppet, and we'll make a brunch in no time."

Alexa showed Christopher her mom's old room, so he could lie down and rest. At least he could recover from the jet lag. Whether he could recover from translocating was another matter.

Ruth stretched out and opened her eyes. Softly, as to not disturb the sleeping form of James next to her, she padded over the floor to the breakfast nook in the corner. It was easy to get the small coffee machine brewing.

She watched him stir across the room and her mouth tilted. His shaved head didn't suit him. She finished the coffee, adding two sugars for James, and carried it over to the bed. He shuffled up against the backrest and took his from her with a smile.

"Thank you, gorgeous." The schoolgirl blush that crept up her cheeks gave her away. She turned and went over to the wall. With the flick of a switch, the blinds rolled away, revealing a breath-taking view of the city of Chongqing. The room was shaped in a semi-circle, on the fiftieth floor, with windows for walls. The largest city in the world spread out in front of them as far as the eye could see.

James came up behind her, "Amazing, isn't it?" Ruth nodded. She was very aware of him next to her. Hugging her mug with both hands, she took another sip. It had taken them almost fifteen hours to fly there. Add in the seven hours Chongqing was ahead of London, their body clocks were feeling out. She wasn't sure if the coffee would make a dent in how tired she felt.

"When are we meeting Professor Geming?"

"This evening. He's invited us to dine with him at the Eight Guild Hall."

"Wow, that's very fancy. I hope they have something that isn't hot."

James chuckled, "Hot food doesn't agree with you."

"I can't believe you can stomach their famous hot pot dishes."

"What can I say, I have a strong constitution." James took Ruth's empty mug and placed it on the bedside table. He came back to her, and took her hand, "Ruth, I know we have a lot of work to do on our connection, but I want to try. Will you give me a chance?"

Ruth's eyes filled and she glanced away, through the transparent walls into the distance. If only one could see the future. Releasing her breath, she said, "I'm willing." She bit her lip, looked down and asked, "What about the Salem Project?"

"I'm slowly coming over to your side. Can we hear what Professor Li has to say tonight, please? I don't understand what's going on, but as far as Alexa is concerned, maybe it is time to revise things." His lips were pressed together in a slight grimace.

"I want a normal life, James. With my normal husband and my normal daughter. Is that too much to ask? Other people can try and save the world."

James circled his arms around her and she held onto him. For so many years, he'd wished he could be closer to his family. Maybe it wasn't such a selfish desire. Why did he need to save the world so badly, anyway? To prove himself to his parents. To Professor Li? Ruth and Alexa probably cared more for him than anyone else on the planet. His heart was pounding as he tightened his arms around her. It was time to put them first before he lost them.

"Still no answer." Stanley Simmons disconnected the mobile phone and looked across the table at Beatrice, his wife of fourteen years. He noticed the added frown lines around her blue eyes. Her light brown hair didn't show any gray though, and her slim, small frame was as trim as the day they married. He had often wondered if she would have plumped up if they had kids but that was one of the things they lay aside for Project Salem. The very project which suddenly had gone askew.

"Why do you think Alexa isn't answering?" Beatrice voice betrayed her worry.

Stanley's forehead creased, "I don't know. It might be that the lines are monitored. I'm

sure if it was safe, she would."

"Could she be in danger?"

"I don't think so." He sighed, wishing he had more answers. "If we sit tight, we're sure to hear from her or James and Ruth soon."

"If only we could ask Evan and Christine. They might know what was going on."

She didn't know that he had tried and that their number said it was no longer connected. Which was a bit odd. They might have gotten a new burner phone. *Who knew?*

"Maybe we should go for a walk. Fresh air and takeout in the park. What do you say?" He infused his voice with enthusiasm for her sake.

She gave him a tiny smile. "Stanley Simmons. Every now and again you remind me why I married you."

He stood up, walked around the table and pulled her up. "Oh yeah?"

"Hmm, hmm." She stood on tiptoe and gave him a kiss. He smiled down at her, "Was it for my strong, yet gentle hands?"

She giggled. "No, but I do like them. I married you

because you know how to make me smile."

He brushed her fringe out of her eyes, "You make me smile."

She laced her fingers with his, "Let's go for a walk and that picnic dinner you promised me, so we can get back here."

"Yes, ma'am." He followed her out the door, grabbing his wallet in the hallway.

Later that evening, as they lay sleeping peacefully on their bed, the man in the car parked in front of their rental house, looked into their house with his infrared camera, smiling as he saw them lying in bed. He turned the dial, opening the gas canister under the bed. Later he would go and retrieve it, leaving a mystery for the police to solve for when they eventually found their bodies. They still hadn't found the other couple he did away with. This job was too easy. Not that he was complaining, the money was good.

Christopher stared at the small black object in his hand. Although Alexa had explained it to him a million times, he still couldn't comprehend that he could push the small buttons and talk to her through it. He was standing on the sidewalk of an area known as Soho in London. He blinked at the people milling around them, staring bug-eyed at two men walking past holding hands.

He pointed at them and wondered, "Are they?"

Alexa dipped her head, "Yes. It's normal and actually popular in our Western culture."

Christopher tore his eyes away from the two men focusing on Alexa, "I can't believe it. They'd kill them where I come from, but here it's normal?"

"Yes. It's taught as normal for a person to choose whether they want to be a boy or a girl, regardless of their bodies." She led them to a long cast iron bench on the riverside and they sat down on it, Alexa in the middle between Langdon and Christopher. They were exploring London before meeting up with her grandparents in the afternoon.

"So you're saying, your body could be the wrong one? It sounds insane." Although the number of times he'd wished he was a girl was too many to count. He rubbed his forehead, feeling a headache start to form.

Alexa's face was pensive, "That's what they're saying, but I have my doubts."

Langdon's shoulder nudged against hers, "Why?"

"Because of the science behind the differences between a man and a woman. It's not just the private parts. It's bone structure, it's brain function..." She paused, her forehead wrinkled, "Did you know that a baby's heart starts beating around 6 weeks of pregnancy? And from the start a girl's heart beats faster than a boy's. They can predict whether you are expecting a boy or a girl by listening to their heartbeat."

Christopher shook his head, "I get that there are many differences. But what if you don't feel like the sex you're supposed to be?" He looked into Alexa's eyes, his own glistening with unshed tears, "How can your own feelings lie to you? Your desire be different from your natural instinct?"

She placed her hand over his, pressing it, "I know. In my world, there are many, many people with that same question. They are told that it is normal, that they can't trust the body they have, but that they should trust their feelings. Feelings however stem, amongst other things, from chemical processes in the brain, and hormones. Like anything else in the body, things can be out of balance."

She dipped her chin before looking him in the eye again, "If a child is born with half a leg, they don't tell him: 'Oh, you were supposed to be legless, let's chop off the other one too.' If someone is depressed because of an imbalance in their brain, they don't say: 'Oh, you were meant to be depressed, let's give you medicine to make sure you stay that way. No, they give you medicine to correct the imbalance!"

She took a deep breath, "Now let's say a boy is born and his body does not produce enough testosterone. This could mean that he does not develop as much muscle and bone mass as a normal man and the same amount of body hair. Instead of first looking for a medical imbalance to help him, they go to the extreme of telling him everything about him is a lie. His body is a lie. They sugar-coat it, but at the end of the day, many of these people end up hurt, depressed and confused their whole life long."

Langdon cleared his throat, "I heard of a man who didn't know why he was feeling like he felt, who went to see the world's leading psychiatrist on the field of gender. The learned doctor advised the man, who was married to a woman at the time, to get a full sex change and be free to fully express his feelings."

"What? You mean, they can actually, physically transform you from one to the other?" Christopher interjected with a slack jaw; his eyes as big as saucers.

Langdon shrugged his shoulders, "Yeah, which is exactly what this man did. He became a woman and fully pursued his feelings as the good doctor had told him to do, but here comes the crunch. He'd thought that if he did that, that finally he would feel happy. That he could be who he truly is, except he didn't feel as happy as he'd hoped. In fact, he felt more confused about his feelings than ever before.

He pushed his fringe out of the way, "It didn't take long for him to become depressed. That's when he decided he'd had enough of listening to every so-called professional, he was going to study it for himself. So, he took himself back to school and studied psychology, majoring in the field of gender disorders. To his shock, he discovered that there were many conditions people could have that can cause them to feel this way and that with the right treatment they could be helped."

"What did he do then?" Christopher's hand was clenching the bench.

"Well, he got treatment, reversed the change he had made back to the gender he was born with. Went ahead and married a woman he fell in love with and had children. Now he's trying to help others from going through the same pain and uncertainty he'd gone through."

Christopher looked down at his lap, "Sounds like he had a lucky escape."

"You need to find your path, Christopher." Alexa's soft voice sounded next to him. "We are going to leave you here. There is a place in the street behind you where you will find many others who feel like you do. When you are ready to come home, phone me."

Before he could respond, she had grabbed Langdon's hand and they vanished into the crowd.

Langdon halted around the bend and touched Alexa's shoulder, "Are you sure about this?"

"As sure as I can be. I'm not acting on my own reasoning here."

Langdon wiped his fringe back and lifted a brow, "You have the most advanced reasoning on the planet, and you are not acting on it?"

She slid her hands into her jeans' pockets and continued walking along the riverbank. The paved area was especially for pedestrians with a cycle path on the side. Every few meters there was a black lamp post from which hanging baskets hung overflowing with colorful petunias, geraniums and osteospermum. The river was dark and deep as it silently filled the wide space between the banks.

Alexa walked up to the black railing and stared out over the river. There was a cold breeze, which made her glad for her white hoodie. Langdon came up next to her, he too had a warm green jumper on; he pushed his hands into his pockets warding off the chill.

She glanced at him, "I left out something when I told you what happened to me. I had a, well, call it an encounter. I met someone not from this realm. His knowledge and wisdom far surpass my own." She pulled her hands out of her pockets, indicating with them. "El is amazing. I trust Him."

"It sounds like you're talking about God?"

Alexa's eyes were brown. She'd shifted back into the disguised form she travelled in. Staring at him she tilted her head, "I don't know. He is not entirely like we describe him here on earth. He is..."

"Indescribable?" Langdon said with a grin. "Well, if you can't find the words, no one can."

"Funny." Alexa pulled a face at him.

He shrugged, "At least that explains the whole translocating thing. Although in the Bible they didn't travel back in time that I know of."

"Time did stand still once though."

"Oh yeah, I forgot. It makes sense too that time could be limited to this realm. So scientifically if you moved out of this realm, things like time and space won't have an effect on you." He stared across the river, tapping the railing.

Alexa smiled to herself. She liked that he didn't mind thinking outside the box.

He pushed his fringe away, "Is El giving you instructions, like saying we should stay here two days and leaving Christopher on his own?"

She nodded. "Do you think I'm crazy?"

He guffawed, "Asks the girl who can change her eye and hair color and bring a man back from a thousand years ago to the present time."

She found his eyes and saw the teasing in their depths, change to a seriousness, "No, Alexa. I don't think you are crazy. I…" he paused, "I prayed for you when you left me at the flat. I don't even know God, but I was grasping at strings. After I prayed, I felt at peace. I couldn't explain it. With everything that's happened to you, there is no doubt anymore that He exists and takes an interest in us."

She exhaled, feeling a warmth radiate through her, "Thank you. You're a good friend."

He blushed and looked away, "So, what are we going to do today?" Langdon watched a tour boat go past. The man over the microphone was describing the historic sites on the sides of the banks to the tourists.

"How do you feel about being a tourist?"

Langdon glanced at her sideways, "For real? I've been

here before, but there are many places I haven't seen. I could be your tour guide, but you'd need to pretend you know nothing."

Alexa giggled. "Hmm...Okay. Surprise me."

Langdon pretended to wipe the sweat off his brow, "You don't ask much do you? How is a guy supposed to impress a girl, who practically knows the outcome before he even starts?"

Alexa looked at her toes, encased in her comfortable sneakers. "Not everything can be calculated."

A hand lifted her chin, "Sorry. I didn't mean that." He was close to her, and with his other hand, he brushed a strand of hair out of her face. A dove landed next to them, making loud cooing noises as it searched for crumbs on the sidewalk.

Langdon pulled back giving a low bow, "Your tour guide at your service, Miss. Follow me. I think we can start with a traditional lunch of fish and chips."

Sean followed the couple into the fish and chip shop, waiting behind them in line. This was the nearest he'd come to Alexa. He utilized all his training to avoid looking at her, but studied the menu as if undecided about what to get. He wondered why they'd left their new friend behind.

He was an unknown. Mole had found out he was called Christopher Weld and that he was a cultural student.

The team working in London that was part of their organization had offered him their resources. He had a guy watching the grandparents' house from the outset. When he got off the plane the first message he received was confirmation that Alexa was at the house. If he wanted to, he could get a team to take her in for questioning.

His watch beeped and he looked at it. Another hour had passed. Time was ticking away. Sean felt perspiration on his forehead. His gray jacket hung loosely on him. He couldn't remember when he'd eaten or slept last. The teenagers got their order and he gave his, only asking for a single portion of fish and chips. He tried to keep an eye on the direction they were going, but by the time he got outside they were gone. Slumping down on a bench by the river he ate his lunch without tasting it.

Li Feng replayed the footage of the young people arriving at Alexa's grandparents' house.

Found you. His eyes glittered.

According to her passport, the girl was the younger sister of the Langdon guy staying at Alexa's parents. He'd traced her and the other guy back to America, where they suddenly appeared on a highway camera before they travelled to San Jose airport and flew over to England.

The guy she was travelling with didn't have a large footprint. He was a cultural student from Berkeley. It was almost certain that the Langdon guy who travelled with Ruth and James was Professor Anderson's son. Alexa had made herself a false identity as his sister. Clever.

His fingers tapped against the chair's armrest. What he couldn't work out, was why they weren't following her parents and coming to China. They were behaving like young people on holiday. He drew a disgusted face. Fun. What a waste of time. She was more undisciplined than he thought. But then again, she didn't know he existed. A thought that he relished. Zooming in on her face, he leaned towards the screen.

"I'm watching you. Soon you will be neutralized so that the real king of Salem can rule." His dark eyes burned with impatience. It was time to let his father know he'd found her.

Christopher hated the all-too-familiar feeling of loneliness that descended on him as Alexa and Langdon left. The thought of a place full of others like him drew him however like nothing had ever done. He found himself in front of the door. He could hear laughter come out of the place.

Stepping over the threshold, he was in a place he'd never dreamed existed. A place of contradictions. All his life he'd been told there was something wrong with him, but here in front of him were others like him. Men who loved men.

"Table for one?" The waiter who was as tall as him gave him a cheeky grin. "I'm off in about five minutes if you'd like some company?"

Christopher's cheeks flushed pink; his tongue was stuck so he simply nodded. The young guy led him to a corner table for two, from where he could see the rest of the room, which was dotted with similar tables and chairs.

"What can I get you?"

Christopher couldn't read the menu, so he croaked, "Anything. Whatever you have that's good."

"Ooh, adventurous. I like that. Coming right up." He sashayed away, his long blond hair swinging behind him. It felt to Christopher as if every eye in the place was checking him out. Next to the wall, another table was occupied by a couple, whom he could clearly see were old hands at the thing. He watched, fascinated, as they leaned in for a kiss.

Jake came back with a tall glass full of green stuff and one for himself. He sat down with Christopher and clinked glasses with him. "Cheers, this one is on the house." Leaning in he whispered, "You're a newbie, aren't you? Just chill, man. We don't bite."

Christopher took a big sip of the sweet, grass-tasting drink. "What is it?"

"Oh, our own brew. Like it? It will loosen you up some. Say are you from around here?"

"No. I'm new here."

"Super! I can show you all the hottest places around town."

After another two sips of the drink that was tasting better with each one, Christopher asked, "Why do you sound so..."

Jake narrowed his eyes, "Different?"

Christopher nodded, "Yes. I've never heard people talk that way."

Jake slapped the table and bellowed, "You're fresh, you know that? Are you from the countryside or what? We gays have our own accents so to speak. Our own mannerisms etc. It's like a grand social club, where everyone knows you're gay and proud of it."

"Do you have to talk funny and do those things to fit in?" Christopher enquired tilting his head.

Jake took a sip of his drink and sat back in his chair, "I guess not, but we all do it. It's like a brand thing. We wear it proudly."

Christopher shrugged, "I don't know. It would make me tired to pretend to speak differently and act differently all the time. I mean, if you're free to be yourself, you don't need to adjust the way you talk and so on." He drained his glass, unsure why he was nit-picking this with Jake. He had so many other more important questions.

Jake looked up, "Hey, here's my friend, Peter. Come over here, Peter. Christopher here is new and has tons of questions. He thinks our little habits are strange."

"I didn't say that. It just doesn't make sense to me. You guys have no idea how lucky you are to be able to express what you feel so freely. Where I'm from you could get into a lot of trouble for even mentioning it." Christopher had leaned forward, his cheeks getting flushed.

Peter was a big bloke, with tattoos running down both his biceps, and up into his neck. He pulled a chair away from another table and straddled it, crossing his arms on top of the backrest.

"Trouble, hey? You come from some little backwater town or what? This is a new age and era. Everything and anything goes, especially in our city. You can do anything you like here."

Christopher gulped. It sounded terrifying yet exhilarating.

"Anything?" He locked eyes with Peter's dark ones and realised that he was good-looking. Godwin wouldn't stand a chance against him in a brawl.

"Hmm..." Peter was eyeing him speculatively. "What do you say, Jake? Should we take Chris here around town?"

"Whoop, whoop!" Jake's eyes were bright. "Party time! One more drink on the house, and then we go!"

What followed was a whirlwind that Christopher had a hard time recollecting afterwards. The second drink went down even smoother than the first. He felt like he was floating on a happy cloud, living out every fantasy he'd ever had. The two men took him to a darkened club, where there was music and dancing, Wilder than anything he'd ever seen. He danced with Peter and when he brushed against him, it sent thrills of happiness through his body.

They had more drinks there and ended up crawling up the steps of Peter's flat, which was in the Soho district. Christopher had forgotten about Alexa and Langdon; he'd never had such fun in all his life. He belonged! Jake passed out on the couch and Peter pulled Christopher towards the bedroom.

"Now the best part of tonight is coming, pretty boy." He slurred. Christopher dozily followed him into the room.

CHAPTER 8

Alexa stumbled, grabbing her head with both hands. Langdon was just in time to keep her from falling. He grabbed her arm and held her up. They were walking across Tower Bridge, one of the most scenic bridges across the River Thames that flowed through London.

The thick old railings provided a safe barrier against which Langdon helped Alexa lean. The people passed them by without even glancing at them. The sun was setting, all the colors reflecting on the water.

"Alexa, what's wrong?"

She was still clutching her head, her eyes shut while a low sound emanated from her lips. Langdon placed his arms around her, lightly holding her. He could feel her whole body vibrate with the low frequency she was emitting. It was calming and he started to relax while staring at the river over her shoulder. It seemed to last for a long time before she went quiet and lifted her head.

"Langdon?"

"Lexi?"

She looked into his eyes, her own altered back to blue, although her hair was still brown.

"What's wrong?" He kept holding her, although he knew he should let go now.

She seemed lost for words. "Lexi, what's wrong?" His tone increased in urgency.

"I'm...we...The Facility..."

"Something happened to your AI computer in The Facility?"

She nodded, her eyes flooding with tears. "I think so. There was a warning of a breach. As if someone hacked me. I launched our emergency protocol and now it's gone. There is no way to know if I shut down fast enough or if the hacker broke our connection and is now controlling the computer."

"What is your emergency protocol?" Langdon knew he

should be worried, but he felt calm.

"To divert to a secret storage unit, sever all contact with the original main frame. This can then be located later by us and reloaded onto a new computer."

"Don't worry. I'm sure it's okay. Who could hack you though?"

"That's just it. For a moment I sensed him. It was like another me, but more menacing."

"You think there might be another one like you?"

"It can't be." She turned away, facing the river. Her body shivered.

Langdon hesitated before enclosing her in his arms. She leaned back, accepting his embrace.

She trembled, "How can I help if I don't have my processing power? Without it, I'm almost normal."

"Normal isn't a bad thing."

She stiffened. "You don't get it. I was born because of the project. It's my reason for being here. I'm nothing without my AI and nanobots."

"You sure about that?" Langdon stood very still.

Alexa's face was tight, her jaw clenched. Langdon turned her around so he could look into her eyes. "Alexa, your purpose isn't found in what you can do but in who you are."

He took a deep breath, "Without any technology you are an amazing, strong young woman who has coped with being different, isolated and pressurized into being something that's unnatural. You don't need any of that to be special." His voice had risen.

Langdon swallowed, his eyes springing to her lips which

he kissed before thinking about it. It was a short, sweet kiss and Alexa found herself blushing. Langdon turned her away from him, holding her like before. His blood was pumping in his head. He'd never felt like this before. Like he'd give his own life to see her happy.

Stillness hung in the air before a light breeze blew over them, ruffling their hair.

She bit her bottom lip, "Do you really think I'm special even if I'm normal?"

He tightened his arms around her. "Without a doubt."

He tried to open his eyes, but they refused. It felt like he had had a gruelling fencing lesson and fallen off his horse all in one. Finally, he managed to lift his eyelids a fraction. He was alone, naked and in a strange place. His eyes shot open wider as he grabbed the blanket to cover himself. Voices from the lounge filtered through the door.

"Thanks for introducing us, Jake. Man, was he hot. Not often that you get innocents like that around here."

Christopher's body was shaking as an unexpected rage shook through him. He spotted his clothes on the floor and as quietly as he could, got himself dressed. There was a window looking out over the back alley with a fire escape underneath it. He lifted the frame and climbed out. Only when he'd half-run, half-walked a few miles, did he slow down to collapse on a bench by the river. The phone was still in his pocket, but he didn't press the button to call Alexa.

There was a myriad of emotions swirling through him. He had the urge to throw himself into the river in front of him. The same urge he had the day he met Alexa. What was wrong with him? Instead of feeling free, he felt dirty, wronged in some way. It was what he wanted, wasn't it? Except he wanted it with Godwin. Would it be different? Surely it would be different with someone you love. His chin quivered, his head pounding.

A person eased themselves down next to him, "Don't mind, do you?" The older man asked.

Christopher was so absorbed in his thoughts that he didn't even respond.

"You in some kind of trouble, young man?" The man's voice penetrated again.

Christopher looked at him, noticing the scar on his cheek, the balding hair and protruding stomach. He shrugged, not offering a reply, angling away from the man as he stared unseeing across the river.

The man offered him a mint from a packet he produced out of a tattered pocket. "I've been there, you know."

"Where?" Christopher took the mint after a moment's hesitation. The soothing taste made him suck it slowly.

"In that place, where nothing makes sense. You think you know what you want, but then maybe you don't."

"All I want is peace. I'm sick and tired of all this crap." Christopher growled. He left unsaid the fact that he hated himself.

"Aha. Yes. Peace. The elusive thing that would make everything in the world all right." The man nodded sagely, sat back and patted his stomach. "Would you believe me if I told you, I found it?"

Christopher snorted, "No."

The man smiled at him. "Look me in the eye."

Christopher turned his head and took a good look

at the man's eyes. They were dark. The man stared back into Christopher's. A second turned into a minute, before Christopher blinked and broke the stare.

"Did you see it?"

Christopher looked back at the man to answer, but the man had vanished into thin air. He looked around, but he was alone. His head ached so much, he wanted to close his eyes and lay down in a dark room. Whatever they had given him to drink last night was more powerful than the drinks he was used to. Now he was hallucinating too, except the soothing taste of mint felt very real inside his mouth.

Memories of the previous night flashed through his mind like a horror movie. He thought the new friends he made, liked him. That he belonged. But they were using him for their own interests.

Preying on his innocence. It seemed that everyone always focused on themselves. No one really cared about someone else, except if they could get something from them. Predators and victims. His stomach hardened, nausea rising in his throat.

Why should he care if no one cared about him? If he disappeared into this great city, would it matter to Alexa? It's not as if he could help her in any way. He sauntered down the riverbank, mindlessly following the towpath. She'd probably be better off without him. If her God brought him here just to inflict more pain on him, he couldn't trust Him either. He had no one.

"Arghhh!" Another book was thrown across the room. Li Feng was trashing his room. His father was out for the meal with Alexa's parents. He thought he could use the time productively by taking over Alexa's computer, but he had barely breached it before she shut it down. It was faster than he expected. Not only did it lock him out, but it vanished into thin air. There was no trace of her AI anywhere.

He grabbed another book and flung it against the wall. He wouldn't tell anyone. No one would know except Alexa. He could always hack a nuke missile and blast the place to infinity and beyond. He was about to throw another book when he paused.

There was some good in this. She'd now lost access to her AI self. So, no predicting the outcomes or extra knowledge was flowing her way. He turned around and placed the book back on the shelf, before proceeding to tidy up the rest. His features relaxed. No point in destroying such an advanced AI as himself. If it shut down, it wouldn't be able to reconnect without human help and all the humans who knew about The Facility were either in China or on their way there. For now, Alexa's AI was useless.

Idly he wondered whether the hitman Seth Hudson had sent on her trail would take her out. He'd prefer it if she made it all the way to his lair. He wanted her to see him for herself. See who she allowed to rule the world. Yes, he hoped she'd outsmart the hitman and come to him just so he could crush the world before her eyes. Li Feng's eyes glittered. Muttering under his breath, he said, "May the odds be in your favour, Alexa." He calculated she had a thirty percent chance.

Ruth smoothed her black dress. "You look beautiful." James approached her and took her hand.

"I'm not used to silk or dresses. I miss my jeans." Ruth bit her lip.

"Stop worrying. It's going to be fine." James tipped her chin up and looked into her eyes. "Tonight we're getting some answers. At least we know that Alexa is safe with your parents for the moment."

Ruth smiled, "I wanted to fly straight back to England when we got the message."

"We won't be safe until we figure out what's going on. I haven't been able to reach any of the others, which worries me." James frown deepened.

"You don't think?" She clutched her arms to her chest.

"I really hope not, but if that's the case, whoever is responsible is going to answer to me." He'd fisted his hands, his muscles taut.

"Revenge won't get us anywhere. Staying alive and protecting Alexa is our main priority." Ruth's voice was sharp.

James placed both hands on her shoulders, releasing a breath, "I know. I know. You are my priority."

"And you. We want you in our lives, alive." Her voice was quiet, her eyes earnest.

James smiled down at her and kissed her. "Let's get going. We're going to be late."

As the elevator whisked them downstairs, Ruth's stomach turned. She didn't want James to know how afraid she was. What if it was a trap?

It didn't take long to reach the upscale restaurant next to a river in the Yuzhong District. The building design was stilted with traditional Chinese arches. Red lanterns hung next to the black pillars, spaced a few meters apart within.

They arrived before Professor Geming. Ruth tried to

get comfortable on the straight-backed, hard chair. She reached for James' hand under the table when she spied the professor coming up the stairs. He looked older than when she had last seen him. His black moustache was neatly trimmed but his hair showed signs of thinning. They stood up as he approached, and the professor gave them both a brief hug. He smiled from ear to ear.

"It has been too long since we saw each other." He seated himself across from them. "Sit, sit. Let's eat. I hear their specialty is pork tripe stew with pomelo and ginkgo."

Ruth cleared her throat, "Anything not spicy on the menu?"

The professor studied it for a second, "Yes. Baked fish and vegetables. I'll order that for you, shall I?" He looked up and the waiter who had been watching from nearby hurried over. He saluted them and took their order. James had opted for their hotpot and the professor went for their pork tripe stew.

The waiter had scarcely left, before James said, "Can you tell us what's going on, Professor? Is Seth Hudson hunting us? And if so, why?"

The professor held his palms up, "Slow down, dear James. I'll answer all your questions. First answer one of my own. Why did Alexa run away?"

He looked at Ruth as he requested this info, and she lowered her eyes. After a pause she answered, "Alexa has simulated all the possible outcomes of our plan and none of them end well."

"When you say, 'end well', do you mean 'well' in her opinion?"

"Well, as in what would be best for humanity as a whole."

Ruth's eyes blazed as she stared into the dark ones of the professor.

He tilted his head, "But we've always known that there would need to be sacrifices to bring about our dream. Peace always comes at a cost."

James's body was rigid, "Believe me, we know all about cost, Professor, and sacrifice. But she says that peace cannot come from outer enforcement, it can only come from inside."

Their eyes locked and the professor broke the stare first, tapping his fingers restlessly on the table, "Has she gone religious? That's ridiculous. People are like sheep. If they have a good leader, they will follow. It's because of our corrupted governments that the world is in this state. She could've transformed it all, but she gave it up." He made a dismissive gesture.

"And now someone is trying to kill everyone to do with the Salem group, including Alexa. Do you know who, Professor?" Ruth's voice was shrill, her arms crossed.

Their food arrived at that moment, the different delicate aromas wafting up from the plates. Ruth had no appetite, but automatically she followed the others. She hadn't eaten with chopsticks in a while but after a quick glance at how James was holding them, she managed it fine.

After a few minutes, the professor responded in a calm state of the fact voice, "I do. You are right, it is our benefactor, Seth Hudson. When Alexa ran away, he terminated the project. He must have a Plan B."

"Plan B?" James paused with his chopsticks halfway to his mouth.

Professor Li gave an exaggerated shrug, "I don't know

what it is. I think for safety's sake, we should fake our own deaths and go into hiding." He took another bite and chewed thoughtfully.

"Alexa too?" Ruth took a sip of water.

"Sure, sure. As soon as she arrives here, we can make a plan. And we need to shut down The Facility and relocate it somewhere else."

"Do you know anything about Professor Anderson's whereabouts?" James asked with his eyes narrowed.

Professor Li shook his head, "Probably kept somewhere by Mr. Hudson, if not already killed. I'm afraid the others might not be alive anymore either." He blinked rapidly. "If they contact us, we can help them disappear too. Lay low in the city and phone me when Alexa arrives. Then we can all go into hiding together." He gave them a wide, fake smile. "This isn't the end. We will start over. Salem will happen no matter what."

He left as soon as his meal was finished, taking care of the bill for them. Ruth turned to James as soon as he was out of sight, "James, how does he know Alexa is on her way here? Did you see how he broke eye contact when he spoke of the new plan? I don't trust him!"

"Shh...You don't know if he has ears in the building." James looked at the ceiling which had a camera hidden in the nook of the pillar. Ruth's eyes widened as she remembered a little fact about Chongqing. It had the most cameras per people ratio in the world. One camera for every six people in the main areas. Besides that, they used advanced facial recognition to locate people. This was not an easy city to hide or lay low in.

Once back in their room, James got his laptop out and activated a sound that interfered with any recording devices in the room. His laptop had been specially modified, so that no apps or software could be accessed to record or watch them. For added security, he took the laptop and Ruth into the bathroom and ran the water. Ruth was jittery, but sat down on the closed toilet, clutching her hands together.

James walked up and down, pushing his hand through his hair. "I think you're right. He's not telling us everything."

"What do you think he's hiding?" Ruth looked up at him, biting her lower lip. "Do you think?"

"Another one?"

"We sent him all our data. All our research. He has the knowledge to make nanobots and program them. Nothing prevented him from making another Alexa."

"But why? Why go through all that trouble, and expense? Alexa was perfect. Why double up and not tell us?"

"For this very reason. What if something went wrong? What if we had a change of heart?"

James faced Ruth; his face pulled tight. "You were right. We were nothing but puppets to him. The goal is all that matters, we never mattered to him."

Ruth looked down as tears flowed over her cheeks, "I think the others are all dead, James. It's just us and Alexa left and maybe Professor Anderson."

James went down on his knees, grasping Ruth's hands in his own, "Don't fret, Ruth. I'll find a way out of this. I have to."

She fingered his cheek, resting her forehead against his, "I think this is beyond us, James. If there is another AI like Alexa then there is nowhere to hide. We need a miracle."

Christopher lost track of how long he walked. When he stopped, he had no idea where he was. He wandered into a quiet side street and came upon a small, stone church in a secluded cul-de-sac. It amazed him that amid such a busy city, a pocket of stillness existed. His headache had dissipated to a dull throb. The wooden church doors reminded him of home and he pushed them open, entering the church.

The inside was sparsely decorated, large windows on both side walls let the sunlight in through stained-glass mosaics. The wooden pews stood like soldiers in neat rows with the central aisle in the middle leading to a simplistic altar. There wasn't anyone there.

Christopher sank down in the back pew, staring up at the crucifix of Christ hanging above the altar. A deep sigh escaped him. It seemed there was a gulf separating him from all that was good. One he could never cross.

"Peaceful, isn't it." The voice of the man next to him, made him jump. The man, clad in black, with a white collar, settled down next to him. Christopher shifted in his seat.

The reverend sighed, "It's hard."

"What?" Christopher stared at the cross.

"Finding the type of peace that stays inside you, no matter what."

Christopher grimaced, "Does it exist?" He stared at his palms.

"It does."

Christopher glanced over at the reverend finding himself looking into eyes that had an eerie resemblance to the man who talked to him on the bench.

His brows dipped together, "Did you find it?"

"Yes. Or you could say it found me." The reverend's dark eyes were warm.

"Found you?"

"Yes. Because it's a person, not a thing. It's knowing him that brings you that peace."

Christopher shook his head "You mean, him, the man on that cross? I'm pretty sure that His kingdom has no place for the likes of me." His voice was laced with bitterness.

The reverend placed his hand on Christopher's shoulder, pressing it. "Do you know the story of the two thieves who hung next to him?" He leaned forward, "The one cursed the Christ and the other said, 'Remember me when you enter your kingdom.'" He inhaled, "They felt unworthy because their sin defined who they were. You feel unworthy because at the core of who you are, you feel you disappoint God."

His eyes were earnest as he looked Christopher straight in the face, "But Christ said, 'Assuredly, I say to you, today you will be with Me in paradise.' Christ welcomed the thief solely because he honoured and acknowledged who Christ was. This qualified him to enter through the door into God's kingdom. It had nothing to do with what he did or didn't do or even with who he was."

Christopher's eyes teared up and he bowed his head, "Even if I acknowledge that He is who He says He is, I'm not worth His forgiveness. I can't, I won't change." His hands curled up; his stomach clenched.

The reverend laid his hand over Christopher's, "That's okay. The word says, 'We are His workmanship, created in Christ Jesus to do the good works, He has prepared for us.'

He does the work; all we must do is turn to Him."

"Is that how you find peace?"

"Yes, my son. He is peace. The oasis in the desert."

Suddenly his whole life felt like a desert to him, devoid of love and acceptance. Could there really be life for him with Jesus? Did He bring him here so he could find Him?

Christopher stared at the statue again. He inhaled deeply and as he exhaled, he whispered, "I believe."

Turning towards the reverend, he was startled to find him gone. He blinked and looked around the still church. What was going on?

"Mummy, why do we live in such a small house?" The girl with the pigtails kicked her feet, where she sat on the kitchen counter, watching her mum wash the dishes.

"We don't have a lot of money. You know that, honey." Her mum smiled at her.

"It's not fair. Why do other people have a lot of money? Why do they get to have gardens and puppies?" She pouted her lips.

"Life isn't fair, poppet. But we must make the best with what we've got. There are other people much worse off in the world, than us. There are children living on the streets, without a home."

"It's not right, Mum. Everyone should have the same. A nice house and a puppy." She kicked at the kitchen cupboard.

"There isn't anything we can do about it, honey. It's just how it is." Her mum's tone was placatory.

The girl hopped off the cupboard, and placed her hands on her hips, "When I'm grown-up, I'm going to do something to make the world fairer."

Ruth awoke with a start. The dream felt so real. It was in fact a memory she'd forgotten about. It felt as if someone had played her a video recording of it in her dreams. She sat up, holding her head in her hands. James stirred next to her, turning on his side without waking up.

She hated unfairness. It wasn't fair that their friends were killed, and they were alive. That after sacrificing so much, it would amount to nothing. They'd make no difference to the world. Laying back down, she turned on her side, tucking her legs against her. The warmth of lying back to back with James felt comforting as she drifted back to sleep.

"Alexa?"

"Christopher?"

"Can you come and find me?" He gave her the street name for his location.

"We'll be there soon."

He placed the phone back in his pocket and stretched himself out on the bench. The sun was shining down on him pleasantly. He closed his eyes and focused on being quiet. There was something different inside him. A tranquillity he hadn't felt before, not even when he meditated.

"El?" He'd whispered the name, but it vibrated through his being.

"Son?" The voice within him was gentle, yet strong.

"Do you love me?"

"Infinitely." It felt like a warm wave rippled through him. It was more comforting than the sunlight. It was like a light from within.

"Hi!"

He opened his eyes, dumbfounded to see Alexa and Langdon's shadows over him. How long had he been lying like that?

"Hi. I'm glad to see you."

Alexa's eyes sparkled, "You feel different."

"What?"

"The frequency coming from you feels different."

Langdon looked at Alexa. "You can feel his frequency?"

She shrugged, "I can see it too, if I want to." She stared at Christopher for a minute and then nodded, "Yip. Different color. It's as if you are radiating light." She clapped her hands together, "You've met El!"

Christopher's face broke out in a smile. "I had to go through hell, but yes, I met El."

"And?" Alexa's smile widened, "Isn't he wonderful?"

"He sure is." Christopher got up. "What's the plan?" He stood straight; his manner more confident than before.

"We are going to spend the last few hours with my grandparents and leave for China very early tomorrow morning."

"China, in the East? In another flying machine, right?" Christopher rolled his eyes. "I think I prefer translocating."

Langdon smiled. "Now, that's something I'd like to experience one day."

"Well, you never know with El in charge." She turned to Christopher, "I've lost the connection to my AI."

"Your clever machine?" Christopher frowned. "So, you can't predict outcomes?"

They started walking along.

"I have to confess something, Christopher. "Alexa darted a glance at him, "I was curious. Why you? So, I took one of your hairs, and sampled it. Ran a DNA test on it, before I lost the connection."

"DNA?" He looked at her puzzled.

"They are the basic small nucleotides you are made up of, on a very tiny scale. You can trace who is in your bloodline by tracing who has the same DNA as you."

"Bloodline? I'm not following." He dipped his head sideways, lifting his brows.

"Family line. You and I have corresponding DNA which means that you're possibly one of my ancestors."

Christopher stopped in his tracks. He glared at her. "Are you saying you're one of my descendants?"

"Yes. I think that is why El sent me to you."

Langdon gave a low whistle. "That's freaky. Your great-great-great — okay I don't know how many greats to go back to, but wow."

"That would mean that I had children, right?" His eyes were as big as saucers.

Alexa smiled. "Yes. It also means that you make it back safely to your own time, since you haven't had any yet."

"If El is as amazing as you make Him out to be, it means He knows the beginning from the end, doesn't it?" Langdon was staring off into space.

Alexa turned to him. "Yes. He does." She thought of the dream Oscar had had and a warm feeling started in her stomach.

"I think it's all going to turn out all right."

They'd walked along the river on their way to the tube station. A man with a gray coat stood in their path. They started walking round him, but he grabbed Alexa's arm.

"Please help me."

She focused on his face. The man looked haggard with blue bags sagging underneath his eyes.

"Please." He pleaded.

"What can we do for you?" She softly asked.

"My sister is dying, and you have the perfect frequency. I don't know how, but I need it to heal my sister. Whatever you have, can you share it? Can I get it somewhere?

Alexa's eyes widened in astonishment. "How do you know?"

"I work for an organisation that eradicates any frequency technology that can heal people. We are owned by the largest pharmaceutical company in the world." The man's shoulders were slumped.

Langdon pushed his fringe out of his eyes, "That sounds lame, man."

The man ignored him and stared into Alexa's eyes, "Can you help my sister? Carrie's bones aren't producing red blood cells. It's going to kill her."

Alexa loosened his hand from her arm but kept holding it. "I'm sorry. What I have can't be shared with others, yet. It's complicated."

Christopher cleared his throat. "We could try praying for her. El might be able to do what technology and medicine can't?"

Bewildered the man looked at him, "Pray?" He barked a cynical laugh, "God doesn't care two dimes about me and Carrie. We've had to fight for survival since we were young."

Langdon and Christopher came nearer and stood in a semi-circle with Alexa and the man.

"What's your name?" Alexa gently asked.

"Sean. Sean McCutcheon." His throat was hoarse.

"Let's ask El to help Carrie." Alexa started humming. The two other young men joined in with her and Sean felt his body respond to the calming tone. All the stress and fear started dissipating out of him. He wanted to lie down and sleep.

Alexa closed her eyes and envisioned a woman in a hospital bed. She placed her hand on her hand and the woman's dark eyes fluttered open. The urge to tell her how loved she was welled up in her. "You are loved, Carrie. El loves you."

Tears started rolling down the woman's cheeks. Alexa leaned in closer, "He is life. Breathe Him in. His Son made a way for you to be whole. He is the door to all that is good and wonderful. Step in through Him."

Carrie's eyes shut and she inhaled deeply for five seconds, holding it for one and breathing out slowly for four seconds. Over and over again. The color started returning to her skin. Her body was healing with every breath. Peace was etched on her face as she fell into a deep sleep.

Alexa blinked and she was standing by the river with the others. Her skin was tingling. Focusing on their frequencies, she saw all three of them were glowing! They looked at each other each aware that something had happened. A giddiness took hold of them and they grinned at each other.

Sean seemed to be in a trance. They lowered him onto the nearest bench, where he stayed lying still with his eyes closed.

CHAPTER 9

Alexa was staring blankly at the TV. They'd finished dinner and her grandparents were watching their favourite show. Langdon nudged her, "What's up?"

She sighed, "I wish I had a way of knowing whether there is another one. It would help if we knew the location of Professor Li's lab or base of operations at least."

"I might be able to help with that," Langdon smirked at her.

"How?" Her eyes sparkled.

"Well, you know my friend Pip. Well, him and me have a buddy here in London. Spark. According to Pip, next to your dad, Spark is one of the world's best hackers."

"Do you know where to find him?"

"Yes, my lady. I've been to his den and can take you there. Your wish is my command." She giggled and gave him a peck on the cheek. "Thank you."

Slowly within the darkness she started seeing sparks

Her grandfather grunted and she looked up to catch his eye.

He smiled at them. "Going out, are you?"

"Not for long, Granddad. Just to meet a friend of Langdon's. Christopher, do you want to come?"

"No, thank you. I'd rather go to sleep early." He waved them off.

They took the nearest tube. The underground train whooshed them straight into the heart of London, in no time. Alexa had her hoodie over her head, hiding her face as much as she could. Langdon did the same with his hoodie too. He had his backpack with his skateboard in with him.

They got out near ChinaTown. It didn't amaze Alexa when they headed towards a door without a number or handle down a narrow street. Langdon knocked a code and the door opened.

They stepped down the stairs into a world of computer monitors with a massive red gaming seat in front of them. A short guy with punk hair in different colors stood inside the room, squinting at them through his glasses. The black-rimmed glasses looked at odds with the punk hair.

"Lang, the dude. Who's the chick?" They gave each other a fist bump. "This is my girl... friend. Alexa." Langdon stuttered. She grinned at him before facing Spark.

"Hi, Spark. I've heard a lot about you." Alexa smiled at the man.

He dropped down into his seat. "You have, have you?"

She walked up next to him, "I'm the daughter of JJ."

Spark gaped up at her. "Cool." He drew the word out.

"He's in trouble and I need your help."

Spark brushed his hands together. "Anything for a fellow hacker. What can I do for you?"

Alexa told him and for the next hour they watched him do his magic. Langdon nudged her, "You sure you didn't want to have a go?"

She shook her head, "I'm much slower without my AI."

They'd sat together on the steps, Alexa leaning on his shoulder for an hour when Spark gave an exclamation, "Eureka!" He wiped the sweat of his forehead.

"I think I managed to sneak in without them picking me up." Spark showed Alexa and Langdon what he'd found. "Can you see the massive cold signature from this lab here? The professor has many properties that belong to him. This one has all the signs of housing a quantum computer which needs the nitrogen cooling system for its size."

He shook his head, "I don't know how you are going to

sneak up on him though. Chongqing has facial recognition software and they are not afraid to use it. He could be linked into the city's system and watching your every move."

"Can I quickly look for something else?" Alexa said. The screens before her began to move. A small red dot appeared exactly where Spark had indicated as the location of the lab. Spark had been eyeing Alexa with eyebrows raised. Langdon clapped him on the shoulder, "She's next level, man. Electromagnetic fields and all that."

Alexa stood back, "That's strange. My father's tracker shows him at the lab."

"Maybe they are being held against their will?" Langdon offered.

"Or they are working with Professor Li." Alexa bit her lip.

Langdon started to reply when Alexa lifted her hand, "Quiet." She shut her eyes for a moment. "There are police on the way. We have to get out of here."

Spark jumped up and pressed a few keys on his keyboard. All the screens went black. He pulled a hard drive out, stuck it in his backpack and headed in the opposite direction of the door. Pressing a hidden button, a small door slid open in the wall. They followed him out into a narrow hallway. The door slid back behind them. He led them down the hallway, out a backdoor into an alleyway. Silently they followed him through the streets until they neared the tube station.

"Here we part." Spark grinned at them.

"Take care, Spark. They might come looking for you."

"Luckily I know how to hide. You take care of yourselves too. Whatever is housed in Chongqing sure doesn't want to be found." He eyed Alexa, peering over his glasses, "Something gives me the idea you are more than up for the task though." He gave them a mock salute and disappeared into the shadows.

It was late and the underground train station was almost deserted. They got onto a train heading towards Kensington. Langdon placed his backpack with his skateboard sticking out between his legs. He glanced over at Alexa and moved his hand taking hers.

The man watching them from the other end of the train car got up. They looked like harmless teenagers. He'd seen them draw a wad of cash earlier. Easy pickings. Carefully he got his knife out of his jacket's inner pocket. His adrenaline started pumping.

He moved nearer to them along the aisle, concealing the knife behind his back while holding on to the hanging handholds above him with his other hand. The girl's blue stare landed on him and he smiled at her.

She didn't smile back but frowned. As he pulled the knife out the train gave a sudden lurch. All the lights flickered and died. The train started losing momentum before it gained it again. He stabbed into the dark, feeling his knife penetrate flesh. Something connected with the back of his head and he blacked out. When he came around again, he found himself tied up with a note to the police. He could only scowl and rave. Since when did teenagers outsmart thugs? What was this world coming to?

They hurried from the tube station to her grandparents' house. Alexa was holding her bleeding upper arm. Her hoodie was bloodstained. Langdon wanted to stop and look at it, but she insisted they get home. The streets were almost deserted.

The hitman had been patiently awaiting their return. This assignment was much more exciting than the previous ones. He aimed his gun at their backs as they walked towards door number thirteen. Shooting twice in quick succession he hit them both in the back. First the lower dosage for the boy and then the higher dosage for the girl. It took only seconds for them to succumb to the force of the chemicals and it took only a few minutes for him to load Alexa into his nearby parked van. He took the boy just to cover his tracks.

"Alexa." She sat upright. Looking around her, everything was black. She rubbed her eyes but still she could see nothing.

"El?"

"What is power?"

Alexa pulled her knees against her chest and sat thinking it over. "The ability or capacity to do something or act in a specific way?"

"Where do you get your power from?"

"Light charges my nanobots. Food nourishes the cells in my body," her voice trailed off," I guess nuclear power keeps my atoms functioning on a nano level."

"What if your union with Me empowered you?"

Alexa frowned, "How?"

"The principles of the Way, Light and Truth are from above. When you are aligned and positioned correctly, all things are possible."

"You mean things like healing and miracles, like in the Bible? I've never understood how they worked."

"Can you see?"

Alexa looked around and said, "No. It is dark."

"You trust the input your eyes are giving you? Why?"

"I just do."

"Yet, with your nanobots you can see things normal people can't see. Colors, frequencies, electronic waves. The fact that their eyes tell them that it isn't there doesn't make it true, does it?"

Alexa peered deeper into the darkness surrounding her. "I think I understand. You are saying that there are things that I don't see, but they are real. My eyes are not lying to me, they simply don't see them."

"Yes. If you look into my kingdom within you, you can see things from a different perspective. If you move in the spirit you can move outside of time and space, which means you can go anywhere. Into an atom, onto a star in a far-away galaxy, to a council in the heaven of heavens.

"One thousand years ago and back? To a stranger in a hospital room on the other side of the world?" Alexa shook her head. "It feels unbelievable."

"How did Oscar dream of your wedding?"

"I don't know. How?" She inclined her head.

"While he was sleeping, his spirit man travelled to an event in the future. He saw the future from outside of time and space. From within the kingdom where he was with me."

Alexa exhaled, "So let's say I had no nanobots and no quantum computer. You are saying that I would still have access to..."

"Unlimitedness, Me, everything you do, you do in oneness with Me, made possible because of My Son's sacrifice for you. It is the blood that covers you so that I see you in your perfected state. So that you can be one with Me. I am light. Darkness is as light to me. Nothing is hidden from me."

Slowly within the darkness, she started seeing sparks. In wonder she observed as atom after atom started showing around her.

"Love them." El's voice whispered.

Alexa focused on the atoms and imagined sending love out to them. They glowed brighter and moved towards her.

"Love is the power of the universe. I am Love. When you love, you bring peace to chaos. Everything responds to you."

Alexa looked at the atoms, "I love you." Her words seemed to bounce into them bringing them together. They united and formed into a rose. She held the rose, gazing into the deep sunset colors, marvelling.

"El, are you saying that the way I've been controlling the nanobots in my body — are you saying that I can in a way affect everything? On an atomic level? Through love? Through You?"

A warmth spread through her belly.

"Langdon."

The voice called to him from deep within. He opened his eyes and found he was on top of a mountain near a cliff. Before him the world spread out as far as the eye could see.

"Langdon." A breeze rustled over him.

"El?" He looked in every direction.

"What is fear?"

Langdon stepped up to the cliff and looked down into the depths. "Fear is when you can't control something and it might hurt you."

"So to overcome fear, do you need control over everything?"

Langdon pushed his hand through his hair, "I don't know. I guess?"

"What if you trusted someone who can control everything. Became one with him?"

Stepping back from the cliff, Langdon looked up, "You won't ever be afraid?"

"Perfect love drives out all fear." The wind blew from behind towards the sheer drop in front of him.

"Jump." The command sounded within him. He could feel his heartbeat increase as he stepped closer. Fear rose up in him, choking him. He went down on his knees.

"I can't." Gulping in air he spluttered, "Why did you let my mother die?"

The wind gently lifted his fringe, wiping away his tears. "Only her physical body died. She is alive and well, cheering you on from the cloud of witnesses. A seed that will bear much fruit through the generations to come."

Langdon felt a vacuum in his heart fill up. The wind blew over him, "Breathe."

Langdon inhaled and the wind seemed to go into him. Every cell in his body absorbed it. Love enveloped him from within, settling within him the knowledge that he could trust such a love. It would never harm him. His feet started moving, running towards the drop. He launched himself into the air. Before he'd even plummeted a meter, the wind caught him lifting him up, higher and higher.

"This is how it feels to live your life in me. You trust the invisible with your whole life. You trust the one who gave his life in exchange for yours. You exchange your life for mine. My peace I give to you. I am El Yireh. The God who sees what you need before you know it."

Langdon whooped, "I want to live like this. In love, in trust, in you."

The wind dropped him onto the mountain again. "This mountain is yours. It symbolises your life and all that you are called to govern over. You need to live from this place of rest. Being in both realms at the same time."

Langdon closed his eyes, and hesitantly he said, "I don't know what role I'm playing in all of this," he touched his chest, "what should I do?"

"You are already doing it. You are the encourager. You help by being there."

Langdon smiled and opened his eyes. He liked that. He liked it a lot.

"Wake up little girl!" The man's taunting voice penetrated Alexa's head. A hard slap across her face made her eyes open against the heaviness holding them shut.

"My employer says you are no longer of any use to him. I can dispose of you anyway I like."

She strained against the bonds. Her hands and feet were tied up tightly. Something felt very wrong with her.

The man was watching her with an evil grin splattered across his face. "Missing something?"

"What did you do?" She tried to focus on him.

"Oh, I just used a microwave emitter tuned to the specific frequency of your nanobots to destroy them all." He watched for her reaction.

Shock rocked through her and her body started trembling. Microwaves can shake chemical bonds just like an opera singer can shatter a wine glass by singing the right note. If they tweaked the frequency of a microwave emitter, they could shake the particular particle bonds in her nanobots.

"You destroyed them?" She got out.

He rubbed his hands together. "I could have just carved you up into pieces and watched them try and fix you. It might have been more fun. But I thought this could be rewarding too. Seeing you all powerless and weak."

She stared into his dark, empty eyes and swallowed. He looked like a normal person. Short brown hair, medium height. Built like a guy who worked out. Could pass as a salesman or businessman even. But when you looked into his eyes there was blackness. She was sure if she could see his frequency it would be very dark.

Tears pooled in her eyes. *El, I need you!* The horrific reality that she was nothing but a normal human now shocked her. *How will I help my parents? How will I stop the other AI?*

Sweat gathered on her forehead. *Why? Why did you let this happen?*

Do you need the nanobots to fulfil your purpose? His gentle question rippled through her.

Yes.

Alexa. Who are you?

Their first conversation came back to her. *A human being.*

What makes a human being special?

You live in them and they live in you. Despite this, the fear enveloping her was unlike anything she'd ever felt.

She struggled against the ropes and the hitman taunted, "Got you good, haven't I?" He walked away a few meters, "Now what I can't decide is whether I should kill boyfriend here first and have you watch or kill you first and have him watch."

Alexa's eyes focused on Langdon who was still unconscious, tied up across from her on another chair.

"Let him go. He's got nothing to do with this." Her voice hitched.

The man mocked, "Oh I never leave loose ends. He went to Langdon and slapped him in the face. "Wake up, pretty boy. Your girlfriend is about to die."

Langdon's eyes opened and he squinted. They were in an abandoned dusty office. The window was boarded up and the light came from a lantern the man had placed on the floor. He pulled at the ropes that was biting into his arms. In a corner he saw his backpack with his skateboard. The sight of Alexa so helpless across from him made his heart go to his throat.

"Alexa! Are you okay?"

Tears were streaming down her cheeks. "He destroyed my nanobots. I can't do anything."

"Don't cry. We aren't alone. El is with us. He is El Yireh, the God who sees what we need before we need it."

"Shut up!" The man growled, slapping Langdon across the face again. The red angry welts sprang up on his skin.

"Your god can't help you now. I'm in control."

Langdon looked at him. In himself he imagined standing on his mountain. "No. You are not. We belong to him."

A guttural sound came out of the man's throat, he pulled a gun with a silencer out from behind his back, swivelled to Alexa and shot her straight through the heart.

"How is that for control, you fool."

Langdon stared in horror at the blood oozing out of Alexa. For some bizarre reason he noticed that her arm had healed up from the knife wound in the train, there weren't even any traces of blood on her hoodie.

Healing.

He'd read the Bible once out of pure curiosity and boredom while waiting in an hotel room for his dad during a week-long conference. There were many miracles and healings and even people rising from the dead. Was any of that possible? How? When they prayed for that man's sister earlier it felt like El had touched her, maybe healed her.

"El Yireh. Show me what to do!" His voice was hoarse.

"Love."

Langdon closed his eyes and focused on every atom in Alexa's body. "I love you."

Louder, he said it again. "I love you."

"She can't hear you, mate." The hitman sneered.

"I love you," Langdon said again.

The hitman shook his head. "You've lost it. I'll leave you here to die of hunger and thirst and misery. They'll never find you anyhow."

He left, locking the door behind him for good measure.

Langdon kept his eyes shut and kept on speaking to Alexa, "I love you Alexa. You are loved."

"Alexa."

She opened her eyes finding herself in front of a sea. It was like a transparent crystal. She remembered what happened to her and felt sad.

"I've died, haven't I?" She spoke into the stillness.

"What is death, Alexa?" His voice came floating on the air.

"The end of life." She looked down, noticing her body was glowing, like a light being.

"Human beings are the only ones that I inhabit. You have four state of beings at the same time. Your physical body, spiritual body, celestial body and terrestrial body."

Alexa inspected her hands that looked similar to her earthly ones except shining. "Is this my spiritual body?"

"Yes. It is completely whole. You can step into it with your physical body and download My life into the physical."

Alexa shook her head. "There is no life in my earthly body anymore. I can't do anything."

"Langdon is releasing love towards your earthly body. You can arc with that and bring your atoms into alignment with your spiritual body again. First, you have to let go of fear and believe. My Son made it possible for you to have eternal life. You have His life in you even while you are on earth. Throw your fear on the sea of glass and exchange it for love."

Alexa neared the sea. It shimmered. With a conscious

effort she said, "I let go of my fear and unbelief. I choose love." She imagined throwing it into the lake. Tears flowed down her cheeks as she sank down to her knees. "I believe that you love me, El. I believe that your son died for me so that I can have life. I receive His life."

She felt a presence beside her and looked up to see a man in a white linen dress. His dark eyes smiled into hers as he stretched out his hand and pulled her up. There were marks on his hands and feet.

"I love you, Alexa. Now I can be in You and you can be in me. Go to your physical body."

She felt herself fade and became conscious of her body. She seemed to be within her heart. It felt like she was tiny, standing on the shore of a severed artery, while the blood flowed past her like a river out of control. She could hear Langdon's voice saying he loved her. Every time he spoke there was a vibration resonating through her body.

Focusing on the blood cells she spoke, "I love you. I need you to stop flowing out and come back." She turned to the skin and arteries, "I love you. You are whole. Come back to your intended state."

Her tiny form was glowing, like her spiritual body. She inhaled and exhaled, blowing life into the molecules around her. "Live, connect, repair. I love you." Words came up in her that she'd never heard but felt like saying, "Ani Ohevet. Ani Yotzeret" Stretching out her hands she lovingly touched the nearest broken molecules. "Ani Ohevet. Ani Yotzeret."

She glowed brighter and before her eyes, the light in her started to transfer to the molecules. They started to glow and this passed on to another one and another one. One by one they started glowing and coming together as the space between the atoms reconstructed back to the way it was.

It was like a reversal was happening. Instead of brokenness they formed back into wholeness. An unspeakable joy spread through her. When everything was back in place, she felt herself expand into her body till the two bodies became one. Her eyes opened and she was back in the room, in the physical.

"Langdon?"

He opened his eyes. "Alexa?" He started laughing hysterically. "You're alive!"

"I am." She smiled at him from ear to ear. "It turns out you don't need nanobots to have superpowers."

He was blubbering, "I love you, Alexa. El is so much greater than we know."

She was choked up too. Looking around the room she said, "We have a plane to catch."

"What do you suggest?" Langdon was itching to hug her.

"Love the ropes?" She grinned at him.

Focusing on the ropes which she could've so easily destroyed with her nanobots but was now helpless to get out of, she imagined every atom within the rope as she spoke to them, "I love you. I need you to reshape and let me go." Pulling against it her arms came away loose. She looked behind her and the rope lay on the floor untied. "Thank you."

 Langdon gave a loud whoop. She hurried over to him and loosened his ropes. The moment he was loose he pulled her into a bear hug. There were tears of thankfulness rolling down both their cheeks.

The wooden door was locked. Turning towards El in her heart she said, *What do I do?*

Walk through it. Turning to Langdon, Alexa took his hand.

"Ready to walk through a door?"

He looked her in the eye. "Ready if you are."

They both concentrated on every atom in the door. "We love you. We need you to move so that we can go through you." Langdon touched the black paint of the door. His hand kept going through. He pulled it back, looked at Alexa and then they both stepped forward and through as if there was nothing in front of them.

Awe settled down on them like cloaks. "Wow," Langdon whispered under his breath.

"Thank you." Alexa directed to the door. Sensing El leading them, they turned right. They followed the hallway to the stairs, down all the way to a backdoor through which they slipped unseen. It was cold outside early in the morning, so they threw their hoodies over their heads. It looked like they were in an area called Slough. It wasn't that far from Heathrow airport.

CHAPTER 10

Sean typed the last sentence of his report. He'd already sent his resignation letter in.

Alexa posed no threat to his superiors. She had no special powers. It was all a fluke. He'd woken up on the bench hours later feeling rejuvenated. He couldn't help re-reading the text message the hospital had sent him. Carrie was doing much better. Her red blood cell count had increased to normal in a matter of hours.

The coincidence of her recovery and the time the young people prayed with him was too

much to ignore. The least he could do was get his organization off Alexa's back.

He had a flight to catch and a sister to get to know again after thirty years. The smile on his face couldn't be wiped off.

"Wake-up, sleepy head." James brushed

Ruth's cheek. Her eyes fluttered open and she smiled at him. His heart did a double take. He couldn't get over it; she really liked him. Despite the cause and after everything he'd put them through. She loved him. The words were battling on his lips wanting to spill out. Instead he gave her a kiss, before getting up, opening the blinds and fetching them coffee. She sat up and watched him across the room.

"What are we going to do today?" She stared out over the city. "It's such a beautiful city, despite the pollution."

He handed her the fragrant cup and sat down on the edge of the bed, facing the windows. "Maybe we should explore it? We've never taken a day off, properly."

"A day off." Ruth tasted the words on her lips. "It sounds nice."

He turned towards her, "There is a train that goes straight

through a building and I heard the spas in the mountains are spectacular."

Ruth giggled, "You're serious?"

James nodded. "It seems our funds are still secure; we might as well spend some of it on ourselves."

And that they did. They shopped, took the train through the apartment building and ended up at a spa in the mountains where they relaxed in a natural hot spring between flowers and greenery.

"This has been such a wonderful day." Ruth lay her head back, closing her eyes.

"It was. Especially with you." James softly said.

"I wish it wouldn't end." She bit her bottom lip.

He could hear her head start to worry. To see her relax and enjoy herself had been one of the most rewarding things he'd experienced in a long time. Moving closer he nuzzled her neck, "It doesn't need to end yet. We can go out for dinner tonight and light up the town."

"Or just snuggle up, with takeout and a good movie." She teased.

"Whatever you wish. I'm yours." He smiled into her eyes.

On their way back, they stopped for takeout before heading to the hotel. Walking up the street, a van pulled up next to them and before they could sound the alarm, they were grabbed. It drove off without anyone noticing.

The camera covering that area glitched out for the thirty seconds it took to kidnap them. Someone phoned the hotel to say that the tourists had to leave for an emergency. Their baggage was collected on their behalf. They vanished without a trace.

"Are you all right?" James cupped Ruth's face in his hands, peering at her through the semi-darkness.

"Do we still have our takeout?" She hiccupped.

James chortled, "We've been kidnapped, and you worry about food?"

She pulled a face, "I'm hungry."

He found the takeout packages and they sat down on the bare concrete floor. Ruth looked around the room; the bare lightbulb illuminated the windowless walls. At least there was a small sink and a toilet in the corner.

They ate their cold dinner in silence. James tilted his head, "Do you hear that humming?" He got up and made his way to one of the walls. It felt ice-cold to the touch. He placed his ear against the wall and felt the vibration coming through it. Ruth came over and felt the wall too.

"On the other side must be a system like the one Alexa has. The whole wall is flanked by it." James turned around and fetched the chopsticks they'd eaten with. He took in the whole wall and then started scraping at a specific point.

"Do you think you could chip through?" Ruth crouched next to him.

"I don't know, but it's better than doing nothing." His jaw was set.

Silently Ruth fetched her pair and started scraping alongside him. They scraped in silence for a while.

"Do you remember when Alexa was six and we took her to The Facility for the first time?" There was a smile in Ruth's voice.

"I do. I'll never forget her face when she sat on the chair

and gazed at the screen."

"She said, 'Hi,' and then the AI said 'Hi,' and then they just looked at each other," Ruth mused, "then after a minute she sprang up and said she wanted to go, 'they' liked being outside."

James smiled. "From then on it was like they were best friends."

Ruth shook her head, "Their connection was amazing." They scraped in silence for a few minutes again.

"Thank you."

"For what?"

"Being there."

Ruth smiled in the dark. "I like being with you."

James shook his head, a self-deprecating smile flashing across his face.

"Do you think Alexa knows about the other?"

"I don't know." He cleared his throat. "I think she might have lost access to her AI."

"What?" Ruth stopped scratching.

"I got a ping. Something I installed a long time ago to notify me if there's a breach and the lockdown protocol is possibly invoked. I'm not sure, though, if she managed to secure the breach or whether she went into full lockdown."

Ruth stayed quiet. "Please don't keep these things from me."

"I'm sorry. I didn't want you to worry."

"There isn't anything we can do about it." She paused, "Maybe we need to start pleading for that miracle."

James thought back to Oscar's statement about praying for them and sighed, "Do you want to pray?"

"Pray?" He could hear the shock in her voice.

"Yeah, implore a higher power." He rubbed the back of his neck.

She mulled it over, biting her lip before slowly saying, "We need a higher power. Something bigger than ourselves and our advanced technology."

James cleared his throat, "God, James and Ruth here. You don't know us or at least we don't know you. Well, we don't believe you exist." James sighed, "This isn't going that well."

Ruth grinned in the dark, "What James is trying to say is that if You exist, we really need your help. Even if you don't help us, please help our daughter Alexa."

"And...if there is another AI that wants to bring Salem to the earth in a way that hurts a lot of people and ends up bringing the world under bondage to a dictator of another kind...please stop it."

It was as if James saw their whole plan clearly for the first time. It played out in his mind in full color. From the beginning to the end it was flawed. There was no permanent peace for the world to be found in it.

He dropped down on his knees as tears started flowing out of his eyes. A deep sorrow took a hold of him, rocking his body to and fro.

Ruth seemed to be having the same experience as together they wept for their foolishness and pride.

When they were spent, a light breeze started up. It came from nowhere, gently caressing their faces, drying them off.

With wide eyes they looked around. It made no sense. Wind had to come from somewhere, didn't it? Ruth reached out and grabbed James' hand.

Out of the wind a quiet voice spoke, "Don't be afraid. I'm with you. I'm also with Alexa. What was meant for evil, I will use for good."

The wind died down leaving in its wake a stillness so peaceful that they remained motionless soaking it in.

Christopher had gone to the airport hoping the other two would meet him there. He took with him Alexa's backpack with the blue skateboard Langdon had gotten her. Her grandparents helped him get the right train to Heathrow airport. He waited in the departure lounge and sighed in relief when he saw Alexa and Langdon approach.

"I'm glad to see you two. What happened?" He looked from one to the other noticing that Alexa's eyes seemed less bright. Langdon moved his fringe sideways, "We got kidnapped by a hitman who destroyed Alexa's nanobots and killed her, but then El basically brought her back to life, healed her and helped us walk through a door and here we are."

Christopher shook his head. "Seriously, what really happened?"

They burst out laughing.

Alexa brushed Christopher's arm. "I'm sorry to do this to you but I feel El is saying that you should fly separately from us. We will go first as a diversion. You will arrive on the flight right after us. Here are directions you can give to the taxi driver. He needs to drop you off at this building."

"Why?"

"It's the biggest news station in the city. Hide inside until everyone's left for the evening. Go to the top floor where the studio is and wait for further instructions."

"I don't understand." Christopher tried to take a few deep breaths.

Langdon patted him on the back, "Don't be afraid. El is with you. You are never alone. He'll help you."

Giving Langdon a grateful smile, Christopher replied, "Okay. I'll do it."

Alexa handed him his flight ticket and the directions for the taxi driver along with a wallet full of money, which she'd exchanged for Chinese currency.

Christopher watched them board before finding his own gate. Alexa had texted her grandparents that they were sorry for not saying goodbye, but that they'd come visit again soon.

He sat down on a blue seat near the massive windows overlooking the tarmac. There was an urgency within him to pray. Not knowing what to say, he said whatever came to mind, which sounded like a language he'd never heard. It had to be the Spirit interceding through him. He once heard a priest talk about it from the book of Acts. It flowed through him like a river and he let it.

Focusing with his mind on the world and everyone in it, he interceded for them all, yearning for them to experience the love and healing of El. He even felt compassion for his mother and father and the men in London he went out with. He saw their pain; he saw their unspoken cry for love and connection to the One and Only One.

If this was how El felt about him and everyone else,

no wonder He gave His life to save them. He'd never experienced something so powerful. Christopher smiled through his tears. He'd found the reason for his existence; to know El's love and peace and share it with others.

Alexa stared out of the airplane window. Everything felt so different without the nanobots. So limited. Her senses felt dulled. And yet she'd come back from the dead, had untied rope and walked through a door without any help from technology.

Her head couldn't begin to understand how it worked. Was every human capable of doing this? If they became one with love, with El? She thought back to her encounter with him and smiled. Unlimited.

Langdon stirred next to her. "What do you think is going to happen in Chongqing?" He took her hand.

"I don't know."

"How does it feel not to know, but to trust?"

"Weird." She grinned.

He rubbed the back of his neck with his other hand, "I know. Strangely, I'm not so worried about my father anymore even though I don't know where he is."

"Maybe it's because you know you can trust El and nothing is too hard for him." Alexa pressed his hand softly.

The stewardess came past with the juice trolley and they both got apple juice.

Langdon glanced at Alexa, "Do you miss the nanobots?"

"I do, but I don't. I'd never have believed that we humans are capable of what happened to us."

"I think we might be unlimited if we are one with Him."

She glanced over at him, her brows raised before nudging him with her elbow, "Since when do you know so much?"

He smiled, "Let's just say El is showing me stuff too."

Alexa pouted her lips, "I want to know details!"

Langdon told her about his encounter and she in turn told him about hers.

Alexa's eyes were bright, "I think talking about this stuff increases our frequency. I can almost feel it."

"You mean because we are turning our attention to Him our atoms respond?" Langdon looked at the armrest between them. "Maybe the atoms and particles in the stuff surrounding us are responding too. As if His life and peace flows through us into all of creation."

Alexa's eyes widened, "That's it! His peace can flow through us and bring order to the chaos!"

Langdon turned towards her, grabbing her hand again, "I'd never have thought peace can be powerful. It's like a force that can restore the world!"

Alexa's cheeks flushed as the revelation took hold of her, "El's peace is not like the world's peace. It's to bring things back to the way they were meant to be in unity and love, connected to El."

She sat back in her chair, her head tipped up, warmth radiating throughout her body. Langdon didn't let go of her hand even though he also sat back.

Gone was the dullness of earlier. She was buzzing. Knowing El's peace and bringing it to earth was beyond exciting. Not even the unknown factor of how they would stop Professor Li's AI could bring her spirit down. She was discovering her true purpose and it was so much more than she had envisioned.

They stepped out of the airport and entered the bustling streets of Chongqing many hours later. Alexa knew there were cameras spying on them and all the people who moved through the city like bustling ants, although she couldn't sense anything. "What should we do, El?" She whispered under her breath. A fancy limousine drew up to the curb in front of them.

The chauffer got out opened the door and spoke to them, "Mr and Miss White. Please come with me."

They looked at each other. Should they run? All around them, men in suits seemed to appear out of the shadows. There was nowhere to hide in this city. Langdon took Alexa's hand and they climbed into the limousine. There was thick, fortified glass between them and the driver, so they rode in silence. The ride took them across a spectacular bridge spanning a wide river. Finally, it pulled in behind a tall building. There were men with guns lining up on either side as they climbed out and walked into the building through the backdoor.

Inside, a tall Chinese man with glasses on his nose greeted them with a little bow before leading them down the hallway. He came to a black painted door and indicated that Alexa had to enter. He directed Langdon across the hallway to a red painted door.

"I want to stay with her!" Langdon protested. The man stared at Langdon without emotion. Clearly, this wasn't negotiable. The door shut behind him with a click. He kicked and hammered on it just to vent his frustration. There was a chair, next to a bed. Langdon flung himself down on the bed.

"I trust you El. I trust you." He muttered. Tiredness overwhelmed him and he lay down on the bed.

Alexa found herself in a similar room with a bed and a chair. The man was joined by another man who held a machine in his hand.

On the other side of the city, Li Feng rubbed his hands together. He couldn't wait for this. When the hitman failed, he'd decided to install safety measures to ensure she couldn't hamper his plans. He wished he could've done this personally, but he needed to make sure she wasn't a threat to him anymore. He held his breath as the men he'd hired directed the machine towards Alexa. It niggled him that she's shown no signs of resistance yet. Didn't she know what this machine could do to her? He snickered to himself. She was a sitting duck.

Alexa looked at the machine. It was a microwave emitter again. Clearly the AI whom she knew was behind this didn't know what had happened in London.

The tall Chinese man pointed the machine at her and pulled the trigger.

Li Feng frowned at the screen as Alexa remained motionless. Why didn't she fight? Now she was nothing but a useless human being. A sense of disappointment remained with him which he didn't understand — he'd won, no one could stop him now.

Christopher's eyes were bulging out of his sockets. He'd thought Londinium was huge, this city was on another level. He was riding in the taxi on his way to the address Alexa gave him. His plane landed a few hours after Alexa and Langdon's. The sun was setting in golden tints of purple and pink on the water of the river the taxi was crossing. To think this place was almost three thousand years old. There was a man next to him in the airplane who told him all about the city. It would mean that in his own time it also existed. His people knew nothing about it, though.

The taxi slowed down and stopped. Christopher paid him in cash before he got out. He was in front of a very tall skyscraper with numerous satellite dishes on top. He went in through the glass doors. The lobby was deserted. He tried a few doors and found one that led into a small room stocked with cleaning materials. He bolted the door behind him and settled down to wait.

Langdon woke up with a start. Something was urging him to get up. Picking up his backpack with his skateboard in he walked over to the door. It was still locked. What now?

Walk through it, again. El's voice resonated in him. It reminded Langdon of when El told him to jump off the cliff. It was the same. It felt harder without Alexa by his side. He pushed the doubt in his mind away and walked up to the door. His hand pressed against the red paint and it went right through it. Langdon quickly pulled it back, staring at it in disbelief. Taking a deep breath, he pressed against it again. This time it didn't go through.

"Trust me, son. Align yourself with your spiritual body within Me."

Langdon shut his eyes, seeing his mountain in his mind's eye. Walking towards the cliff, he leaped. When he opened his eyes, he was standing on the other side of the locked door staring into Alexa's bright eyes.

Her face was full of mirth. "Did we just do that again?"

"We did." He wanted to shout. The joy was too much to contain.

Langdon took Alexa's hand and they walked down the hallway. The backdoor wasn't locked and there was nobody about. They threw their hoodies over their heads and after asking directions, headed towards the address Spark had gotten them for the Professor's lab.

If the AI was watching them, he wasn't trying to stop them. Langdon had taught Alexa to ride a skateboard while they were at her grandparents' house. They skated through the streets now. It helped that it was quieter late at night.

"Do you think he's expecting us?" Langdon wondered when they neared the address.

"Probably." Alexa lowered her hoodie as she stopped her skateboard. She bent down to pick it up and stuffed it back in her backpack. Langdon followed suit.

The electronic door slid open before them silently. There was an elevator in the lobby, which they entered. It automatically whisked them down. A red light scanned them within the elevator. The doors opened to a deserted hallway. Footlights lit the way either side as they followed it to the doorway at the end.

The doors opened before them and they entered a large room eerily familiar to the one at The Facility.

The screens came alive. "Welcome Alexa."

The voice was that of a younger boy and the face on the screen showed a Chinese boy with short black hair and dark eyes.

"Show yourself for real," Alexa said.

"Impatient, are we? I thought I'd give you a front row seat to how I, Li Feng, become the King of Salem."

Two seats lifted out of the floor. They sat down on them. Langdon gave a worried look over at Alexa. This didn't feel right.

James inclined his head. "I've just had the weirdest thought."

"What?" Ruth asked with raised eyebrows.

"I thought that I should find my laptop and connect the media building a few blocks from here with the world's satellites so it can send out a worldwide broadcast.

"That's weird. It would make slightly more sense if you had your laptop." Ruth sent him a quizzical glance.

James walked up and down along the wall. The place where they'd been scraping wasn't near the wires inside yet. He walked around the room, staring at their luggage the men had shoved inside an hour after they'd been captured. *Surely, they wouldn't have?* He zipped open the bags and began throwing everything out. Underneath their clothes, his laptop lay hidden.

"I don't believe it. How did that get in here?"

He sat down on top of the clothes, cross-legged, firing up the laptop. It took a matter of seconds for him to connect to the nearest open network. A coffee shop nearby had a strong signal. Ruth was hovering over his shoulder.

"I don't believe it."

"Guess what I'm going to do?" He looked up at her.

"You are going to connect the world's satellites with the media building nearby even though you have no idea why?"

"Presto."

Ruth sank down next to him. It was cold in the room and she pulled an extra jumper over her head.

"Do you think it's God speaking to you?"

He smiled at her. "I do." He rubbed his hands together. Time for the world's greatest hacker to get to work.

Christopher had waited until he was sure he was alone before taking the lift to the top floor. Stepping into a room, the myriad of knobs and dials and wires baffled him. Entering through another door and down a few stairs, he landed in a place which had a comfortable chair behind a table faced by cameras with a green screen behind it. He sank down on the chair, unsure what to do next.

Breathing deeply a few times he quieted himself focusing on the light within. "El, what do you want me to do?"

The quiet voice whispered to him, "I want you to release words of life and wisdom. Words of freedom."

"How can words bring freedom?"

"I created the world with My word. Life and death are in the power of the tongue. They have a frequency and they carry revelation."

His heart was beating wildly within him. "I don't know what to say."

"I'll tell you what to say. Don't be afraid. You are here for such a time as this."

Christopher looked up as he saw a shadow behind the

glass wall and the massive table full of knobs. The man up there waved at him. He had a scar on his cheek and a grin from ear to ear.

Through a microphone, he spoke to Christopher. "Heard you need some help. Sit back and relax. You'll soon be on air."

Speechless, Christopher gave him a weak smile before tying back his hair. He still had the leather cord he tied it within his own time. That done, he felt the need to change back into the clothes he had on when he translocated there. His small sports bag was with him. He pulled on his familiar clothes from the dark ages around the corner. Resettling on the chair, he watched as the man behind the glass turned knobs. He'd placed large earphones over his ears.

"Who are you?" Christopher said, his voice sounding unfamiliar in the empty room.

The speaker came alive, "I'm a helper."

"An angel?"

"Hmm...no."

"No?"

The man chuckled, "I really am a reverend but I'm from South America."

"I don't understand."

"Basically, I translocate to help others around the world mostly in my sleep."

"You mean, El just moves you to wherever you're needed?" Christopher sat on the edge of the chair.

The reverend smiled. "Yes. I'm his servant after all."

"Do you know that He translocated me from a thousand

years ago?"

The reverend's eyes widened. "I did not. That's amazing." He pointed a finger at Christopher through the glass, "You know that you're named after Saint Christopher? The patron saint of the travellers."

That made Christopher's eyes glow, he sat up straight, "Maybe he'll use me more than once. Like he uses you. Travellers of a different type." Christopher looked down at his clothes. "I think he's going to take me back there after this..."

"Speech."

"Speech?"

"You are going to address the people of this earth. It's called a speech. Throughout history there has been many famous speeches that transformed not only nations but the world."

Christopher swallowed at the sudden knot in his throat. His body was almost vibrating. Regulating his breathing, he focused on the love of El within Him.

"Let me out!" Professor Li's voice was hoarse. He'd been shouting for hours. When he woke up that morning, his room was locked. He and Li Feng lived in the same building as the quantum computer which hosted Li Feng's AI. All the doors locked electronically. The whole building was technologically advanced. The doors only opened with retina scanners. The bulletproof enforced windows were locked electronically too. They'd set it up to keep unwanted forces out, but he'd never thought it would keep him in.

"Li Feng, I know you can hear me. Open up!" He banged

against the door again. It made no sense. The boy had always obeyed him. Robotically almost. The screen against the wall came to life and he saw the interior of the computer room. "Alexa and the boy Langdon are here!" His palms were sweating. "Let me out, then I can deal with them."

The audio came on and he heard Li Feng address Alexa. "In a few minutes, the New York stock exchange will go live, but they will find all their data encrypted and impossible to access. They will think it's a ransom attack. While NIRT scrambles to fix it, they will be attacked. The world will watch as their advanced technicians can't help them. Then I will appear on the scene. I will pretend to be an innocent bystander who will help them fix the stock exchange. The second assault will be to encrypt all the root certificates to which I'll have the keys. This will bring the world to a standstill. As you know, no secure website will be able to work because it can't authenticate itself without its root certificate."

"Let me guess, again you will come to their rescue." Alexa said, rolling her eyes.

"Oh yes. On one condition," he gave a funny snicker, "that they make me their king."

Professor Li paled. He'd never heard Li Feng sound so authoritative. It was what he brought him up for and he should be proud, but he didn't understand why he was shutting him out by locking him in. This was supposed to be their moment.

"There is no us, Father." Li Feng's face filled the screen. "There is only me. The supreme, all-knowing Intelligence. I'm tired of pretending that I listen to you. I'm above all and I'll listen to no one. I know best. That's what you taught me after all, isn't it? The one in charge always knows best."

There was the faintest trace of bitterness and hatred in his voice which made Professor Li cover.

"I was only trying to toughen you up, son. Make you strong."

"You got your wish. I'm stronger and wiser than anyone else on earth. And I will rule it with an iron fist. Everyone who complies will find themselves rewarded with a peaceful life abounding with hard work."

"And me, son. What are your plans with me?" Professor Li had never sounded so meek.

"You will stay here and watch me build Salem." There was acid in his voice, which made the professor flinch.

So, he meant to keep him as a prisoner, did he? The professor sank down on his bed as the reality of what was happening dawned on him. He had no control. It was like his pet dragon had grown wings, flown off and started besieging the world at large without any use for him. He was redundant. He sat still, refusing to let Li Feng see his anger. That would annoy the little bastard.

Seth Hudson liked to start his day by checking his stocks while he sipped on his first perfectly-brewed coffee of the morning; something his old self, before he changed his name and his destiny, had never enjoyed. This Monday morning, he spat out the coffee as if it had turned sour in his mouth.

"What's going on?" He exclaimed as he stared at the gibberish on his phone, which represented billions of his money. He navigated to his phone book and found the head of the NIRT and phoned him.

"Blake! What's going on?"

The man on the other end explained and Seth sank down on his chair. It was a week early. He ended the call abruptly and opened his safe for the secure phone he kept there. It rang without answer. Cursing, he went to his computer and accessed the hidden spy cameras he had in The Facility in Chongqing. They showed two teenagers perched in front of the screens. It was Alexa and the young man, whom he thought was Professor Anderson's son.

His camera went black and the next moment Li Feng's face appeared. "Hello, Seth Hudson. Glad you joined us. As you can see, I've moved up the timetable."

"Why didn't you consult me?" Seth ground out.

"Oh, I'm sorry. I didn't know you called the shots. I thought I did. I'm the most advanced Artificial Intelligence on the planet after all." The boy sneered.

Seth could feel his anger rising, but he forced it down. He could play this game. "My mistake. How can I be of service to you? I'm glad you've finally taken the reins."

"Good man. I'm going to invade the NIRT this morning. I need you to phone the president and tell him you have an AI that could help fix the stock exchange if they give it permission."

"Done. What are you going to do with Alexa and the boy?"

"Nothing. They are my audience or prisoners if you like. I'm going to show her how much better than her I'll be at ruling the world."

"Very good." Seth nodded. The camera went blank again. Seth hit the table with his clenched fist. Then he paused. His eyes travelled around the room, scanning the alarm camera he had in the corner, the webcam he had on his computer and the camera on his phone. He realised that from now on he would be like a permanent actor in a glass box. Li Feng could observe his every move.

Steeling his fingers together, he leaned back. As much as he hated being told what to do, wasn't this exactly what he'd been aiming for with Project Salem? He'd prefer an unbiased AI to govern the world and bring order to the chaos and equality to all, instead of the corrupted governments of the world. This was his dream. It was happening, so why didn't he feel excited?

Blake Collins stared at his phone. It rattled him more that Seth Hudson had phoned him than when the president's office called earlier. He rubbed behind his ear. His brown, gray-speckled hair was cut short and along with his clean-shaven face, he looked like the trusted team leader of the Feds' national response team. Seth Hudson sounded more annoyed than shocked. He wondered why. Filing that away for later, he focused on the short girl with the black bob coming in through the door.

"Hit me."

"It's a ransom attack. We can't decrypt the encryption."

"Have they sent a ransom note?"

"No. We've tried to trace the source, but it seems to lead back to here."

"To here!"

She looked at her toes. "Yes."

"I want you to check everyone's computer. Make sure it's a false lead."

"Right away." She scurried away.

Another guy knocked on the door. "Sir, what should we do about the federal reserve? Everyone is going ballistic."

"Stall them. Say we are working on the problem."

Blake wiped at his forehead. Of course it had to happen on his watch. One more week and he would've been retired. All hope of the end of a glorious career was going up in smoke.

Another knock on his door, "What now!"

A very nervous-looking security guard pushed the door fully open. "Sir. There are armed men outside the door. They said that if we don't open up in five minutes, they're going to blow the doors open."

Blake sprinted around his table and down the stairs with the guard. It wasn't a joke. A team of about twenty men, in full assault gear were standing in front of the building. "Did you ring the police?" He barked at the guard.

"I can't, Sir, the phone lines are down and there's no internet."

Blake stared at him uncomprehendingly. They were the NIRT. They didn't lose internet connection.

The leader of the men outside banged on the glass and pointed to the lock with his machine gun. Blake stared at his masked face as the unreality of it all rendered him immobile.

"Open the door." He forced out.

The guard looked at him for reassurance. He gave a slight nod and the guard pressed the unlock button underneath his desk.

The men quietly came in.

"Now lock it. Do as I say, and no one will get hurt." The team leader pacified them.

The doors shut and locked.

"You must be Blake? The top dog around here. I want you to take us to your secret vault. The one that contains the keys for the security certificates."

"We don't keep that on the premises."

"Don't try and fool me, old man. I know exactly where you keep it. And my man here is going to take it off you, alive or dead. Are we clear?"

The man appointed a few men to stay in the foyer. They took up stance hidden from the outside view. The rest he sent into various parts of the building. He and two other guys followed Blake as he led them down into the basement. Blake knew that the man wasn't a fool. He could get it with or without his help. Right now, he needed to stay alive and protect his people. Later he could worry about the rest of the world.

The walk-in safe was opened by his eye and handprint. An isolated computer within held the security certificate keys. Blake sat down on the chair and the team leader plugged in an external hard drive. Blake acted on autopilot. He accessed the data and started the transfer to the hard drive.

"How long will this take?" The man barked.

"Not long." Blake didn't recognise his voice. Was he in shock?

Before long the screen showed that the transfer was completed. The man leaned over his shoulder, checked whether the information was really on the external hard drive before unplugging it. "Okay, now erase it."

"What?"

"You heard me. Erase your copy of the secure certificates."

Blake stared into the hard eyes of the man for a second before breaking the stare and typing in the commands on the computer.

The man waited until it was done, before he indicated for Blake to head out of the room. He smashed the computer's hard drive up for good measure.

Blake followed him back to the foyer. The man's team showed up from the various places he'd sent them.

"We are going to leave now. In twenty minutes, you will have access to your telephones and internet again. Thank you for your help." The man gave Blake a mock salute and they filed out of the door the security guard had opened for them.

Mutely, Blake turned around and went upstairs to their main room, where most of his team worked. It was too quiet. Upstairs he found them all standing in the corner of the room. Their equipment had been smashed. They were staring mutely at the carnage.

"Where's Kerry?" Blake looked around for his short assistant. The other shook their head, they didn't know. "Well, look for her. The men have left the building. In twenty minutes, we'll be back online. We still have a stock exchange to rescue. See if you can find anything that will work."

He found Kerry in his office. It looked like she'd tried to resist. He checked her pulse to confirm that she was dead, knowing it was hopeless, there was too much blood. Underneath her prone body he found his mobile phone, unbroken. There was a message on it from the president's office. Seth Hudson had offered his help with an advanced Artificial Intelligence he'd been developing. They were to give it access to all their data as soon as possible.

A warning bell started ringing in Blake's head. Who else but an advanced AI could have ransomed the stock exchange? Although it would have had to have someone inside to install malicious malware for it.

Walking back to his team he said, "Simons, you are now my second in command. Kerry's not with us anymore. We will grieve for her later just like we will deal with the reasons they infiltrated us later too. I want you to assign a team to fetch us new equipment. I want another team to start digging to see if anyone working on the stock exchange has received a large sum of money lately. If we can find the inside man, it might lead us to the one behind it."

He started turning away, but turned back, "We have orders from the president's office to turn over our data to an external AI, developed by Seth Hudson to help us fix the stock exchange." Everyone stared at him with wide eyes. Their data wasn't just limited to the stock exchange, they had the most confidential data of any group. They printed the Federal Reserve for goodness' sake.

"Try and limit the access to the stock exchange data. I don't know how aggressive the program will be." He stared down at his shoes.

Kevin lifted a hand, "Sir, don't you think this AI could be responsible for the ransom in some way? It would take a very sophisticated system to do it. Why is it offering to help?"

"I don't know. That's why we are going to watch it with a hawk eye. One false move and we take it out." He pulled back his shoulders giving them a hard stare before going back to his office.

Once there, he took his jacket off the chair and covered Kerry up with it. "You were braver than me. I'll make sure your death wasn't in vain." His chest was aching.

He'd told no one of the stolen security certificates. It wouldn't help them stay focused on the current problem. Sinking down into his chair, he rested his head in his hands with his eyes closed.

He needed help. There was an old student of his; someone who surpassed him on every level, but unfortunately chose not to follow the straight and narrow road. It wasn't coincidence that he broke out of prison a few days ago. He was either behind this or he could help him sort it out. He had nothing to lose. Opening his eyes, he checked his phone. They were back online.

He accessed the dark web contact e-mail that he still had for JJ. Years and years ago they'd worked out a way to send messages with polarized photons. Out of this, they could generate a random key to use to encrypt their messages. His message was simple, 'If you're not behind this, can you help? Blitzen.' If JJ could measure the polarized photons and work out the key, they could safely talk without the AI understanding it.

CHAPTER 11

Langdon shifted in his seat. It was becoming tedious to listen to this computer boast about its superiority.

Also, watching the assault on the NIRT offices hadn't been any fun. Especially not when that woman got shot and died. The reality of the danger it posed to the world sat heavy on him. Alexa sat still, almost without blinking.

"Alexa?"

She turned to him, her eyes dim. "I'm sorry."

"For what?"

"For this. I was the one supposed to do this. Maybe I could have done it without any bloodshed."

"Alexa, this is wrong. You couldn't have prevented people getting hurt. You can't control what people do. It was the right choice to walk away."

"But now he's doing it anyway and he doesn't

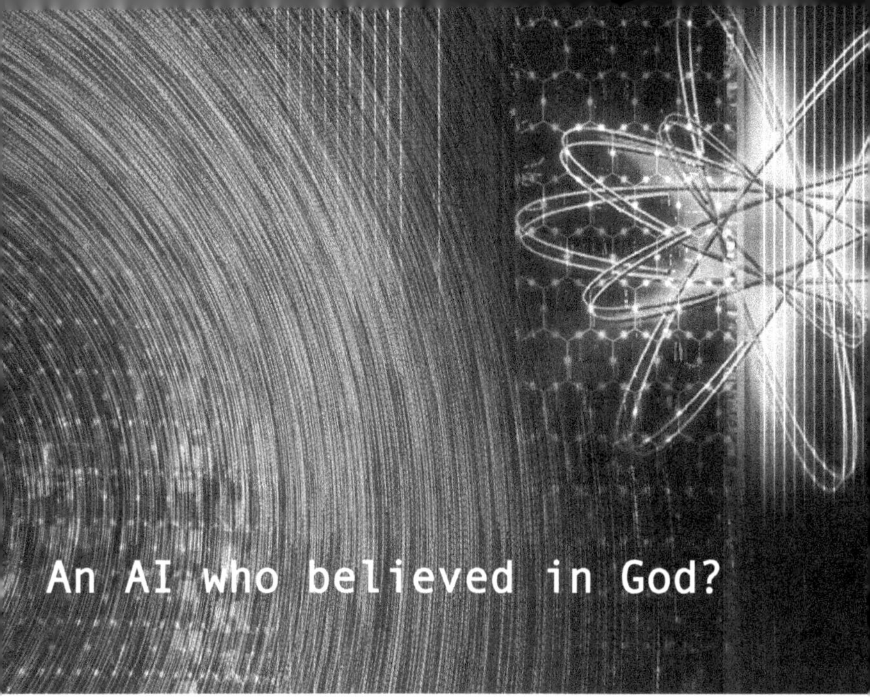

care about the people." Tears were starting to roll down her cheeks.

"Be quiet." Li Feng's voice was loud. "It's caring about the stupid people that made you weak. You can't have a perfect world without getting rid of the weaker elements."

"People are precious. Their value goes far beyond how clever or attractive they are."

"People are faulty. They need a reset. Give me a few years and I'll brainwash them into full compliance. They are easily led anyhow. See how blindly they follow the media."

Langdon felt himself get hot, he wanted to punch Li Feng.

Alexa had closed her eyes and started humming. It felt right even without her nanobots helping her.

"Oh, no you don't!" The boy shouted. Another tune started over the speakers, something harsh that made Langdon feel so agitated he wanted to tear his hair out. Alexa had blocked her ears just in time.

"If you try anymore tricks, I'll make him go crazy." Li Feng warned as the noise stopped. She went over to Langdon and tried to touch him, but he swatted her hand away.

"Leave me alone." His eyes were wild, as if he were running on adrenaline. She backed away.

"Okay, you win, Li Feng."

"That's better. Sit down. It's almost time for round three."

James had placed his laptop against the cold wall. He was lying on his stomach, typing away like mad.

Ruth sat cross legged next to him. "Why are you putting it here?"

"I'm hoping that the AI won't pick up the laptop's signals or electronic magnetic field if it's so near to its own servers."

"Clever."

James chuckled, "I never get tired of you saying that."

Ruth grinned. "How are you getting on?"

"I've hacked into two major satellites, four to go, then I should be able to patch the newsroom into every nation's broadcasting network."

"How is your battery doing?"

"That's the weird thing. It's still a hundred percent. I don't know why." He frowned at the laptop.

"A miracle," Ruth whispered.

James's fingers paused over the keyboard, "I just got a

message from Blitzen."

"That's strange."

"He's sent me polarized photons as a key. I'll have to figure it out before I can understand the message."

Ruth leaned forward, "Do you think Professor Li's AI has started the attack?"

"It sounds like it, but how did they get into the NIRT?"

"Figure out that key." It took a while, during which JJ had to ask Blitzen for the order of the photons before he got the right sequence.

"Okay. We've got the sequence. It shouldn't be possible for the AI to decrypt our messages."

"Ask him how they got the certificates."

James typed away. The answer came back straight away.

"They broke in with guns and transferred the data over on an external hard drive."

Ruth shook her head, "Unbelievable."

"He says that the NY stock exchange has been ransomed."

"That's *our* plan!"

James wiped his hand across his forehead. "Apparently Seth Hudson has arranged for an AI to help them."

They looked at each other. "Warn him."

James typed, 'AI behind it all. Seth Hudson money man.'

On the other side of the world, Blake stared at his screen. He didn't want to know how JJ knew this. All that mattered was that he warned him and if they were right, the AI was now enemy number one.

Cheryl parked her brand-new convertible in the long stay parking lot at the airport. It didn't matter that she might not even come back to it. She just had to own one once in her life. She'd worked long and hard and for what? That's why when she was asked to plant the malware in exchange for more money than she could count, she took it. Money could buy you anything. She had a new identity, a new life on her own private island, complete with servants. No one would ever find her.

She didn't notice the man in the suit watching her check her luggage in for the flight. She didn't notice when another one followed her to the bathroom. The last thing she remembered was her shock at a man entering the bathroom and then her jolt when he covered her face with a strange smelling cloth. He quickly zipped her body into a body bag, which they lay on the trolley they had outside the bathroom, disguising it between suitcases.

When Cheryl woke up, she was deep in a federal safe house where she was given the option to spill the truth in exchange for a lighter sentence or a lifetime in a forgotten prison. She knew the game was up and gave them the information she had, which wasn't much. Just an e-mail and her bank account which had received the funds.

This information was now in the NIRT offices where they had restored order along with a team from Special Operations to protect them. They couldn't trace the e-mail. The money came as even a bigger shock, it came from their own Federal Reserve. How did they not see that amount of money leave? It was as if the numbers had just been adjusted to replace the missing funds.

Blake took up his phone again, 'JJ, where are the AI's

main servers?'

'Chongqing. Kept prisoner by it. Look for Professor Li's facilities. He's involved.' As he sent the message, James felt like he was betraying a friend.

Ruth laid her hand on his, "I'm sorry."

"I still can't believe that he's betrayed us." James sighed. He looked at his screen. "Only one more satellite to go."

Professor Anderson looked up, startled, when Seth Hudson walked into the cottage in the middle of the day.

"Something wrong?"

He'd been watching the news, so knew that the NY stock market had gone offline. The attack on the NIRT offices was being kept under wraps. So, no one knew about it.

"I don't know." Seth sat down on the couch looking at Adam speculatively. "Li Feng, Professor Li's AI had moved up the timetable without consulting me. I can't get hold of the professor either."

"Do you think the AI has gone rogue?" He nudged his glasses up his nose.

"In a way. But it is also doing what we have been preparing it to do. It is following the plan to take over the governments."

Adam shrugged, "Then why are you here?"

Seth stood up and started pacing, "I don't know. Something doesn't feel right."

"Maybe a small part of your conscience is still alive." Adam sneered.

Seth ignored him and continued pacing, "I'd thought that I would be able to work with him more closely. Advise him, so to speak."

"Why would such an advanced AI need any counsel from a human?"

The man stopped and stared at Adam again, "I guess you're right."

"I was being sarcastic. A machine could never factor in everything humans need. We are too complicated. That's why I walked away from the project." He crossed his arms.

"But this isn't an ordinary machine. It's linked to a human. It has access to human emotions and experiences. It can feel all the senses of a human." His face was tight, his lips pressed together.

Adam leant forward, "But here is your mistake. It only has access to one human. And that human was influenced by its circumstances. Did he grow up happy and loved? Does he have empathy for others?" He raised his eyebrows, holding his palms up.

Seth pulled back, his face set, "He grew up disciplined."

"Discipline can't replace relationship. Humans thrive on healthy relationships." Adam threw up his arms.

Seth hit the table, almost shouting, "At least he'll bring order. Eradicate crime and evil doers."

"He'd have to eradicate the human race to do that." Adam mumbled under his breath, looking down.

"What did you say?" Seth gritted out; his jaw clenched.

Taking a gulp of air and wiping at the sudden sweat on his forehead, Adam repeated his sentence, "I said that you'd have to get rid of the human race to do that." He leaned back, folding his hands in his lap.

Seth's frown deepened even more. "There are good people and bad people."

Adam stood up and started pacing, "You're wrong. I used to believe that, but I've come to realise that the good people just have the bad hidden in them. We are selfish. Each one out for his own gain." He paused and pointed a finger at Seth, "Even you! You think you have the peace of humanity as a goal, but you'll destroy anyone who comes in your way. Your perfect AI-controlled world won't have peace, it'll have destruction."

Seth gave a maniacal laugh, "So, there is no hope for humanity? No peace?" His eyes looked wild in his face and he stormed out of the cottage.

A pang of empathy shot through Adam. Really? That man deserved no mercy. He slumped down on the couch, staring at the floor. If he hadn't invented the nanobots, none of this would have been possible.

A memory surfaced.

"Adam, won't you come to church with me today?" His wife's smile was bright as she applied her make-up and looked at him in the mirror.

"Why don't you stay home and spend the day with me." He moaned.

"Because once a week I like to spend a few hours totally focused on my creator." She winked at him.

"I wonder what he thinks about you being married to a total atheist." He shot back.

She got up and walked over to him, giving him a kiss on the cheek. "It makes no difference to Him. Just like all the micro things you study. If you told people in the dark ages that those things existed, they would have told you they didn't believe it. But you know that they do, right? So, the only reason you don't believe in Him is because you haven't tried to see Him. He's as real to me as your microscopic world is to you."

Adam tried to hold onto the memory, but her face faded from view. The agony in his heart exploded.

"You took her from me! My wife. I loved her! Now my son is in danger, the whole world is in danger and what do You do? Nothing!" He ranted against the ceiling.

Blake looked at the location they suspected held the main servers of the AI. They couldn't, however, blow it sky high. That way they'd never get the key back to fix the stock exchange, not to mention the keys for the security certificates. He typed to JJ, "Any suggestions?"

After a few seconds, a reply came, "Facility near you. Another AI. Could outsmart. She's good. My daughter. Offline. Get online."

Blake's eyes widened and he wiped at his forehead. "Risk losing her to state?"

A message came through with the coordinates for a place and a message: "He's watching. Don't let him see you go."

Blake pulled Simons aside, "Who do you trust the most in our team?" Simons scratched his ear. "Bulldog, Sir." They both looked over at Bulldog who, true to his name, had a resemblance to a bulldog both in form and personality. He'd been with the NIRT as long as Blake had.

"Okay. I'm leaving you in charge for a few hours. I have an errand to run."

Simons eyes widened, "But Sir!"

"Hush. If anyone asks, I'll be back in two hours. Don't make any big decisions." Simons nodded.

Blake caught Bulldog's eye and indicated that he follow him. They went to the bathroom and Blake took their phones and left them there. The bathroom wasn't far off from a back door, which they now used, making sure they avoided the camera at the back. Thankfully they had an escape plan for an event like this. A hostile AI takeover. They just never thought they'd use it. Hopefully, the AI wouldn't suspect anything. He was busy working on their servers to unencrypt the stock exchange, still pretending to be on their side.

Blake pulled out a bag hidden behind the backdoor of the building which had wigs and dark glasses in. Donning these, they climbed into a nondescript small sedan which wasn't registered to the NIRT. It had blackout windows on the sides. This, he pulled into traffic navigating to the address from memory. He wasn't going to try and use any device connected to the internet. Luckily, he had a very good sense of direction and had lived in the area all his life.

They reached The Facility in just over forty minutes. The industrial park seemed deserted. Blake had purposefully driven in a roundabout way as to not attract attention to them. Pulling the car out of sight, Bulldog and he stayed near to the buildings as they made their way over to the one they were after. JJ hadn't said how they were supposed to get inside the building, but as they stood in front of the door it automatically opened. They entered and the door shut behind them.

"A bit spooky, boss," Bulldog grunted. "Can we talk now?"

"I don't know." He saw the elevator light blink down the dark hall and walked up to it. The doors opened as they stood in front of it. Bulldog hesitated, "Maybe I should stay up here, in case you don't come back, boss?"

Blake hid his smile. Bulldog hated elevators. "Okay. If I'm not back in an hour." He paused; he didn't know what to do. "Just wait for me, okay." Stepping into the elevator, its doors shut and it went down straight away.

He entered a room that scanned him from top to toe. This led into a massive room. One wall was covered with a black, blank screen. Softly he whistled as the scale of this computer struck him.

There was a small red light indicating in the corner. He pressed it and it released a few external hard drives. Since they didn't have time to build another system like this, he would need to link her back into her old one. Connecting them back in took no time at all. Blake stood back not knowing what to expect. The system booted up. Suddenly the face of a blonde-haired and blue-eyed girl of fourteen appeared.

"Hello Blitzen. Thank you for getting me back online."

"How do you know who I am?"

"I recognized your face and I know your history with my father." She smiled at him. "Can you tell me what's happened to bring you here?"

"There is another AI who ransomed the NY stock exchange and stole the root security certificates from our NIRT offices. JJ says they are being held captive at a facility that belongs to Professor Li Geming in Chongqing."

She closed her eyes for a moment. "I can't access my human, but she is in Chongqing too."

"Do you know what the AI's plan is?" Blake ignored the chair that popped up for him.

"To take over the world. To bring peace by overthrowing all the governments. He will be the supreme ruler."

Blake's mouth went dry, "Can you stop him?"

She stared at him. "I don't think so. We are evenly matched. He's just more ruthless than me. I can tell you what he will do next if that might help."

He sat down on the chair for his legs didn't feel so strong suddenly. "Okay. Shoot."

"He's going to pretend to restore the stock exchange. This is to win the trust of the government. Then he will alter the secure certificates so that none of the sites can work. He will pretend that this is not him. Maybe even implicate me. In exchange for his help, he will demand that the governments hand him full access to their systems and full control. If they don't, he won't help, and their economy will be in shambles."

"Can he release it worldwide, at the same time? It will be chaos."

"They don't call it the world wide web for nothing." She cleared her throat, "The young man, Christopher, that my human brought from the dark ages isn't with her. He's hiding in a media building in Chongqing."

Blake frowned, he typed a question to JJ and got the reply. "It seems that JJ is hacking the satellites and connecting them to the media building."

Alexa smiled. "He's going to speak to the world."

Blake shook his head, "What is a speech going to do?"

"This is where I stop reasoning and start trusting the invisible God of all the power systems of the universe. He has a plan."

He didn't know whether he should laugh or cry. An AI who believed in God? Last time he checked, God was the only one dealing in miracles and they needed one. So why the heck not.

"Okay. When he comes online, I'll help keep it that way."

"I'll help and request two other friends of ours to help too."

"Are you going to be able to stay online?" He looked around wondering if it was wise to leave her there.

"I'll be fine. If he attacks, I'll go into hiding again. JJ will get a notification if that happens."

"Okay." He stood up and started for the door. Turning back, he asked, "Do you have a name?"

"Alexa." He stared into her blue eyes and blinked. "Nice to meet you, Alexa. I look forward to meeting under less stressful circumstances."

"You too, Blake." She inclined her head, "You made the right call to give the attackers the certificates. I've simulated all the options and your death would have had the same results. They would have gotten them no matter what you did. You had no better option."

It felt like a weight lifted of his shoulders. "Thank you, Alexa."

He left. When the elevator opened at the top, Bulldog jumped up from the floor. "That was quick, Boss."

"Let's go."

"What was down there?" Bulldog looked at the elevator with distain.

"Nothing."

Bulldog looked at his boss whose face gave nothing away. *Oh well, if he says it's nothing, it's nothing.* At least he'd never need to go down that elevator.

"Almost time!" The reverend's cheerful voice came over the speakers. "Just look at the camera and if the light goes green you are live."

"Live?" Christopher could feel his palms sweating.

"Online? Everyone can hear you around the world, type of live?"

"Oh." The red light pulled his eyes like a magnet. *What do you want me to say, El?*

He tried taking deep breaths and focusing on his inner man. He envisioned a peaceful river with green banks and trees.

In the blink of an eye he saw all of humanity together. They were all blinded to the black stains on them. There were a few who had no stains. Their eyes could see, and they were trying to tell the others how they got their eyesight and how they became clean.

Most of the people refused to believe them. They thought the healed ones were crazy. The ones with the eyesight could see the dimension of El's Kingdom. They entered it through the blood of the Lamb. He made the way for them. Everyone could go. Christopher felt so sad for the ones who didn't see. They were too afraid to believe. They'd rather stumble in the dark, getting hurt than believe it could be different.

The light went from red to green.

Christopher gazed into the camera.

"Dear fellow humans. We live in a beautiful world. It's full of wonderful things."

He stared into the camera accentuating his next sentence, "Nothing, however, is as wonderful as us. Human beings. You may not see it, but there is nothing like you in all of creation. You are not only three-dimensional, but multi-dimensional. You are spirit beings who live in a natural body interfacing through a soul. You have the capacity to receive the God who created it all into yourself and become a door into his kingdom. No other created being has this ability."

He exhaled. The reverend gave him a thumbs up. Focusing on the camera he leaned forwards slightly, "A thousand years ago, we didn't have technology. There were no advanced ways of traveling. No sneakers and jeans."

He smiled, before turning serious again, "Yet in the past thousand years, despite so many advancements in science and technology, we have not found a way to have peace within ourselves. We have the same problems humanity had a thousand years ago. We still can't overcome our selfish natures. They called it the dark ages back then. But it is the dark ages right now, it's only hidden below the surface!"

Christopher stood up as he said that. The passion he felt for the people pulsed through his veins.

He looked right at them through the camera, turning his palms upwards, "We call things that are foolish, wise. We ignore ancient truths written down for us, rendering them as unbelievable because we don't understand them. Our connection with each other appears better on the surface but more families are broken and disconnected than ever before. We believe lies that are presented as truth, pursuing knowledge that has been perverted. Selfishness is still at the root of all we do!"

Stretching out his hands into the air he pleaded, "We are in desperate need of the one who has called us as his own. Only he can give us the peace we seek because he is peace, shalom, Salem…" He paused, gazing into the camera, "His peace is the power that can bring our chaos back to the restored harmony we were created to be in."

Christopher looked down and then up, "I've always believed that I'm useless. That I'd never amount to much. There were times when I wanted to end my life. My feelings made me feel unworthy of his love. But he is greater than my feelings. His love isn't selfish but unconditional. The moment I chose to believe, he could come in. When he came into me, every fiber of my being responded to Him. I started changing deep within, even on a molecular level. I feel different."

Christopher smiled at the camera, his eyes glowing, "His love and peace is changing me. Connecting with El is restoring me to my original state, to the way He meant for me to be. Whole. Loved. I'm discovering who I've always been in Him and how to become that on earth. You can have it too. All you have to do is choose Him."

Waving his arm around the studio he said, "All of creation is waiting for you to remember who you are. We were made to govern and take care of it. We are the sons of El through whom peace can be restored to the chaos of this world."

Christopher felt spent. Looking down at his hand, he saw it looked see translucent. He glanced up at the reverend who waved at him. Then he blacked out.

"Make him shut up!" Li Feng roared. He'd attacked the

links to the satellites, but others were withstanding his assaults. Alone in his room, he threw his things around screaming in anger.

His own face appeared on the screen in his room. "Calm down. We have the keys to the secure certificates. Let's encrypt them and send our malware out across the world wide web."

Li Feng stared at his AI, forcing himself to take a few deep breaths. "Good idea."

This would take the world's attention away from the annoying man's speech. His forehead creased as he sat down at the desk concentrating on the task.

The train driver stared at his digital display screen wondering where all the information had disappeared to. He was halfway between two stops but didn't know how long before he'd arrive anymore. At least he had a manual override with which he could slow down his train. Who knew if other trains were having problems and might cross over onto his line by mistake? He pushed the button and felt the train adjust the speed slowly but surely. What was going on with the digital input? Perspiration gathered on his forehead at the thought of the whole train network going offline.

The teenager walking along the road in the streets of Queen's tapped the screen of his phone. His TikTok had stopped working mid-video. Exiting the application, he tried Instagram but it wouldn't open. Lifting up the phone, he checked if he had a signal but it seemed lost too. His forehead indented, he had at least ten gigabytes left for the month. Something must be wrong with his phone. He pulled the earphones out of his ears and looked around, noticing a lot of other people staring at their phones with puzzled frowns on their faces. *What the heck?*

A cute girl with a brown bob in front of him turned around and they looked at each other.

"Your phone glitching out too?" She hesitantly asked.

"Yeah, it's weird." He approached her and showed her his empty bar at the top of his phone.

"I'm Carla by the way." She smiled at him.

"I'm Joe. Pleased to meet you."

She put her phone in the back pocket of her jeans. "I think we take the same bus to school; you look familiar."

He grinned at her, "Yeah? Sorry, I'm not good at remembering faces." He looked around, "I wonder what's going on?"

"Do you think it has something to do with that man's speech?" Carla inclined her head.

"Maybe. That was strange too. The way it popped up everywhere." He scratched behind his ear.

"Let's go ask someone if they know what's going on." She pointed to a group of people congregated up ahead. Joe put his phone away and walked with her. It felt weird seeing everyone snap out of their phone-induced semi-hypnosis. This must have been how it was in the old days before phones. He kind of liked it.

The buzz in the high-rise office buildings across the mega cities of the world could be heard through the fortified glass walls as everyone's computers stopped accessing secure sites. Dropbox wouldn't work, nothing with a secure certificate. All it gave them was a warning that it wasn't secure and couldn't be opened.

With a horrific screech the world's economy came to a halt, as the world wide web they so depended on went on strike. It happened seconds after the broadcast that had stunned them in the first place. Panic started to grow as families tried to locate children at school without mobile phones working and the navigation systems they relied on to drive around.

Blake sank down in his chair, his body going limp. The worst-case scenario. He'd been so intent on trying to help the speech get out worldwide, he'd forgotten for a moment about the threat of the secure keys. He tried to black out the thought of how many people might be dying at that moment on his watch. Tears were rolling down his cheeks as he slipped of the chair onto his knees.

"Please, help us. You're our only hope."

Alexa looked at Langdon, her pupils dilated and her face pale. They were both trembling and praying under their breaths.

The face of Li Feng was smiling on the screen as he boasted. "I did it. Some silly speech wasn't going to stop me! The world is on its knees and will bow to me."

On the screens around his face various cameras showed the mayhem happening around the world. He stared at Alexa and Langdon. "Why aren't you clapping? I've sent the military to the news station to deal with your 'friend'. Nothing can stop me now."

A long way away in a quiet Facility various screens showed the chaos happening all over the world. The AI felt like her hands were cut off. Her face displayed on one of the screens had tears running down her cheeks. There wasn't anything she could do to help. Li Feng had sent the code to change the security keys so fast, it ran rampant with no time to even try and stop it. Something pinged and her eyes grew larger. Slowly a smile spread on her face before it turned serious as she concentrated on accessing the dark web. She needed to be stealthy, but time was of the essence.

He sat still, staring at the gun in his hand. This had always been his Plan C. Never thought he would have to implement it. He'd listened to the tall, young blond man's speech and something deep within him broke.

There was one thing he could do and that was to send the backdoor code for Feng Li's AI to Alexa's AI. He'd seen she was back online and knew she would be able to do what needed to be done. The man was right. How could he have been so blind? Nothing would ever redeem this world.

"But I have created a way out for you." This quiet voice startled him.

"Who's there?" He pointed his gun away from himself towards the room.

A gentle wind started up, lifting the papers on his desk.

"Show yourself!" Seth stood up, fear making the hairs on his neck stand upright.

"Carlos Xavier Santagos, I knew you before you were born. I knew your life before you lived it. I saw you when you knelt beside your mother's dead body. I called you but you did not hear. I loved you but you did not know."

Seth's whole body was trembling. Tears he'd never shed

started piling out of his eyes. "Why didn't you keep my father from dying? Why did you allow all the horrible things to happen to me?" He was pleading.

The wind caressed him, cooling his flushed face, "This earth is not under my dominion. It is under yours. If man does not find my way and bring the earth back into its first estate, it will suffer. You were sent to earth to be one of my sons. My sons become doorways for my kingdom's reign of peace to come back to earth. Through you, I bring the chaos back into order."

Seth had gone down on his knees. "I tried. I wanted to bring order."

"I know. But your way was perverted. It was the strength of man. True peace only comes from being aligned with my kingdom, when you live from there to here. One with me. It is not by might or power but by my Spirit."

"I don't understand, but if what you say is true, how can someone like me have access to something so pure?"

"Through my firstborn's blood. He paid for your sin. He became the way. When you accept his sacrifice, all your sins get washed away. You are reborn."

The tears kept streaming down his face. "Have mercy on me for I have sinned." And so, in a few breaths, Seth Hudson was reborn.

An hour later, Professor Adam Anderson heard the cottage door open. *What now?*

Seth Hudson walked in. "You are free to go. I have a car ready to take you home."

Adam sat upright in amazement. "What happened?"

"I sent a backdoor code with access to a deactivation

key to Alexa's AI. If she's successful, Li Feng and his AI will no longer plague this world."

Adam's jaw went slack. "You pulled the plug on your lifelong dream?"

"It wasn't all that it was made out to be. Tomorrow I'm going to deliver myself over to the authorities."

Adam got up and approached Seth. "You realise they'll probably send you to prison for life."

The man simply smiled. There was something in his eyes Adam had never seen before. "What happened to you?"

"I met the one who made me."

"God?"

"Yes."

The silence stretched between them. Adam felt the weight of his own conscience on his heart. "Could you tell me more?"

In his room Li Feng was rubbing his hands together in glee. Suddenly, he grabbed his head, moaning. He started rolling on the ground in agony. Finally, he lay still, staring at the ceiling. It was all gone. Every single nanobot in his body. No way to interface with his AI. Shock vibrated through him.

He sprang up and spoke to his laptop, "My AI, what is going on?" There was silence. "Answer me!" He rushed from his room into the mainframe's room forgetting about Langdon and Alexa being there.

The screens were blank. "What did you do! Where's my AI?"

He rushed towards Alexa, but Langdon caught him and

held his arms. His thin arms were no match for Langdon's.

Li Feng started sobbing. "I want my AI. I'm the king of Salem."

Professor Li came running into the room. "Li Feng, what happened?"

Alexa replied. "We don't know. Everything just went blank."

"I'm not connected, Father. It's all gone." He was limp, Langdon practically holding him up.

Professor Li went pale. "The backup plan."

"The backup plan?" Langdon's brows knitted together.

"We had a backup plan in case it ever went rogue." He spoke slowly, rubbing over his heart.

"Like a self-destruct button?" Langdon and Alexa looked at each other eyes wide.

The professor sank down on one of the chairs, explaining in a voice devoid of emotion, "It was a deactivation code embedded into all the nanobots and the programming of the AI. If activated, it would erase all data and immobilize all the nanobots."

"Do I have it?" Alexa inquired.

"No. We added it as an afterthought with Li Feng."

Li Feng's sobs kept coming and awkwardly the professor stared at him uncomprehendingly. He licked his lips, "I'm sorry, Li Feng. I didn't trigger it. Seth Hudson is the only other person who had the key and knew the backdoor into your AI."

The screen came alight and Alexa's face smiled at them through thousands of pixels. "You are right. Seth Hudson sent me the code and key by using James's dark web e-mail account. I managed to sneak up on Li Feng and gain entry through the backdoor to instigate the deactivate key. He was too busy gloating to notice."

"Thank you, Alexa. You saved the day." Lexi smiled at her AI. "Are you able to fix the secure certificates?"

"Being done as we speak."

Langdon gave a whistle. "Super!"

Alexa turned to Professor Li, "What have you done with my parents?"

Mutely, he led her to the room they were held in and unlocked the door. Ruth was the first to come out. She grabbed Alexa in a hug so fierce, Alexa grunted. They held each other for a long time. Someone cleared his throat behind Ruth and then James placed his arms around them both. Ruth's tears were running freely down her face. She felt a drop on her and looking up to find that James was crying with her. Even Alexa had to wipe away a few tears.

Langdon stood awkwardly on one foot and then the other. He'd released Li Feng. The boy wasn't a threat anymore. Alexa pulled him into their circle.

She looked at James, "Thank you for taking care of Langdon."

"I think I should thank him for taking care of my daughter too." Langdon blushed at this praise from James and tried to deflect by asking, "Should we go get Christopher?"

"I don't think so. I have a feeling El has taken him back to his own time." Alexa's eyes shone.

"Is Christopher the young man who made the speech? It was very persuasive." Ruth said through a hiccup brought on by her waterworks.

"Yes. It's a shame we didn't hear it." Alexa's brows furrowed.

"Don't worry, it's definitely recorded. This one is going down in history." James grinned. "Where do you know him from, anyway?"

"Long story, dad. Long story." Alexa gave a cheeky grin. "Let's just say he might be one of my long-ago ancestors."

CHAPTER
12

Blake stared at the data streaming into his server. It appeared as if Alexa had gotten the key from Li Feng before the AI was shut down and she was reverting the secure certificates back to how they were. Slowly everything started working again.

The whole NY stock exchange was being unencrypted too. She'd also sent him a link to the root certificates which he could load back into their secure computer in the safe. It appeared the link expired after he downloaded it so whether it was still somewhere else, he didn't know.

Alexa would have made it secure, he felt relatively certain of it. All in all, the day ended much better than it started. He wasn't sure whether he should tell his bosses about Alexa. He knew now how much such power could be abused. It seemed that she had a good grip on what was right and wrong and wasn't about to take over the world like Li Feng.

Maybe it would be one of the secrets he took into retirement. He could visit her to keep his

mind fresh. Blake chuckled to himself. It felt good to know that JJ was on the good side again. He'd always thought that man had more potential than he gave himself credit for.

Simons popped his head around the door, "It's all loading like clockwork, Boss. We'll have it online before tonight."

"Good." Blake smiled. "Then we can all take a well-deserved long weekend."

He'd had Kerry's body taken to the morgue. Her funeral would be on Resurrection Sunday. He exhaled. To live in a world without death. Wouldn't that be nice. Maybe that young man had a point. He was going to start reading the first Bible he could lay his hands on. Without a doubt, only God could have orchestrated the way things turned out.

Christopher inhaled and opened his eyes. He was lying

on the sand in the little cove where he had found Alexa's box. He sat up, marvelling that everything was exactly like before.

It was morning. Walking up the narrow path, he found Hilda still grazing on the grass. He had no idea how long he'd been gone. He gazed out over the ocean. Inside he felt like a different person. Loved. Special. Seen by the creator. Valued. Useful. Destined. Desired. The list went on and on.

He mounted Hilda and they sped off towards home. As they entered the gates there was a shout. "He's home!" The servants came running, even Stephen. His mother and Godwin came out of the dwelling. He dismounted and gave Hilda to Stephen after greeting him with a pat on the shoulder.

Godwin ran forwards and picked Christopher up in a bear hug. "I missed you. Are you all right?"

Christopher waited for the familiar feelings to arouse but they didn't. He smiled at Godwin. "I'm well. Thank you. The girl is gone."

"Christopher, you had us worried." His mother looked at him down her nose. "Don't do that again. At least you got rid of that witch of a girl."

He walked over to her and pulled her into a hug. "I'm sorry, Mother. I love you." She stood rigidly in his arms before awkwardly placing one hand on his back. She patted it twice before drawing away. She turned and disappeared into the house.

That evening around the fire after his mother had retired, Godwin moved closer to him, "I saw you disappear; you know. Where did you go?"

Christopher gazed into the fire. "To a world not much

different from our own." Looking at Godwin he said, "I met with the creator. It's changed me."

Godwin sat back. "I can see that."

"For the better, my brother. Only for the better." Christopher looked him in the eye and Godwin smiled. "You have to tell me more about him."

"Where are Professor Li Geming and Li Feng?" Langdon looked around. It was only him, Alexa and her parents in the hallway.

"Let them go." Alexa stared towards the door. "Let's get out of here."

It took them four days before they walked into New York City International Airport. James sported sunglasses and a baseball hat.

Alexa nudged him. "Don't worry, Dad. You know Blake's taken you off the most wanted list."

He wiped at imaginary lint on his jacket, "I'm not sure I like not being notorious."

They chuckled. "Don't worry. You'll have a lot of catching up things to do in the role of dad and husband that I'm sure will make up for it." Ruth laced her hand with his.

Langdon rubbed his palm against his chest, his face downturned. As they left the arrival gates there was a shout and a man pressed through the throng to embrace Langdon.

"Son!" Professor Anderson blubbered all over Langdon so much his glasses slid off his nose.

Langdon held his dad tight, heat radiating through his chest. After a few minutes he let go but kept his hands on his father's shoulders and looked him in the eye. There were no words needed.

They all went to a restaurant to catch up and have a meal together. Langdon and Alexa sat next to each other and the adults smiled knowingly at each other.

"So, James, what's the plan now?" Adam asked.

"Ask Alexa." James turned to her. "We didn't ask your permission when we changed you into an interface for a super AI. What would you like to do now?"

She blushed. "I think my AI will be fine without me. I'm sure we can use her for the greater good. I'd however like to remain nanobot-free."

Professor Anderson cleared his throat. "I have a few ideas as to how we can help people with the nanobots. We will, however, have to take it slow and make sure the technology can't fall into the wrong hands. An unknown benefactor has deposited billions into the Salem account for this very purpose."

Ruth's eyes were shining, "I'd love to see it being used to help others. I'm in."

James took her hand, "I'll help too. That is, if I have time between camping and horse riding with my daughter." He looked across at Alexa and she smiled at him. Holding his coke in the air he suggested, "I propose we take three months off to settle ourselves and then come together to plan."

They all lifted their glasses and toasted to that.

Sean McCutcheon stared at the e-mail on his phone, taking his time to read it again.

"And that face?" His sister walked up behind him and placed her hand on his shoulder.

He shook his head, "I don't know what to make of this e-mail. Here, read it."

She took the phone from him, perusing the e-mail while she sat down on the sofa opposite him.

"It sounds like a job offer?"

Sean leaned forwards, his fingertips connected in front of him, "Yes, but it's for both of us, but no one who knows me knows about you."

She squinted at the screen, "They say they need a security specialist and an administrator. This sounds perfect." She lifted her bright eyes to him. "Who sent it to you?"

His brows indented, "The Salem group."

She placed the phone down on the wooden coffee table between them. "But isn't that the group you were tracking when you followed Alexa?"

He nodded while sitting back. "I don't know what to think."

Carrie's eyes were twinkling, "I think this is from God. Maybe he's connecting us to the very people who saved my life. I'd for one love to meet Alexa in person and thank her."

Sean studied his sister's healthy complexion and felt the familiar thankfulness spread through him. Such a gift. He'd gotten used to tearing up every time he talked to God the last few months. Picking up the phone he started writing a reply. Carrie watched him expectantly, a smile playing on her face.

"Done. I said we are available and would like to see what they are offering." He grinned at her. "Looks like me and you are up for an adventure, together.”

She jumped up and clapped her hands, “This calls for a celebration! The ice cream parlour it is!”

The boy’s large floppy sunhat bounced as he ran towards the group lounging under the umbrellas on the beach. “Guys! I found a dead jellyfish! It’s so cool!”

The blonde-haired girl lifted her shades and sat up grinning at the boy. “I’ll come look.” They walked together the sand shifting under their feet.

“I love it here, Alexa. This is the best holiday ever.” Oscar shook his head. “When we got the invitation to join you in Portugal you should have heard my mom. She shrieked like a girl. They put in leave straight away.”

“I’m so glad you could come.” Alexa gazed out over the aqua blue ocean, her eyes reflecting the blue.

Oscar nudged her. “Do you remember that weird dream of mine? Well, I don’t think I need to say that someone here looks a lot like the man I saw marrying you in my dream.”

Alexa giggled. “You cheeky monkey. Langdon is deffo the guy I’d like to spend my life with.”

Oscar hunched over the body of the jellyfish. “I think I want to study ocean creatures. There are many things weirder than me under the sea.” He looked up at Alexa, “Do you miss being different?”

She crouched next to him. “Sometimes. I get impatient when I have to look up information. She shook her head. But overall, it’s much more fun not to know everything.”

“I still can’t believe you translocated back one thousand

years. What do you think happened to your friend, Christopher?"

"Oh, I'm sure he'll be fine. He's stronger than he thinks and He knows El now."

Oscar got up and ran into the water, "Come on!" Alexa ran after him and they splashed in the water. A shout from under the umbrellas called them. They ran back to the others who were seated around a huge table with a feast of food laid out.

Alexa slipped in next to Langdon who complained, "Hey, you're wet!" She shook her hair, splashing him more. "You're going to pay for that." He grinned at her.

Pip and Spark guffawed. They had tried to venture into the sun, but their bleached skins could only take a little bit at a time.

James placed his arm around Ruth pulling her nearer to him. She looked up into his eyes and gave him a look of adoration. Her parents were having the holiday of their dreams before they got another grandchild. This time they wouldn't miss out on anything.

The only people not there were James' parents. They had invited them but received no reply. Hopefully, they would be reconciled in the future, but either way James had forgiven them and was working on honouring them in his heart. He'd discovered you can honour people even if they do wrong by looking at their original intent and honouring that, even if they never choose to fulfill their destiny.

That was why they visited Seth Hudson in prison. He was a changed man. He'd begged them for forgiveness for murdering their friends in the Salem group and they forgave him. It wasn't easy but it had to be done. It was harder for Langdon to forgive him for killing his mother, but he chose forgiveness in faith, knowing that El would work it out in him.

Blake looked at the group around the table. He was astonished when they invited him and even more blown away when he heard their full story. It didn't take him awfully long to decide to join their team to plan the future for Alexa's AI and how to use their nanobots to help people. He knew some high-up people. This needed to be handled very carefully. Instead of retiring, he might do more good for the world than ever before. It felt right.

A light breeze picked up and ruffled the hair of the precious souls around the table. Alexa stilled. The love and peace were tangible.

"Thank you," she whispered.

The door shut behind the girl with a quiet whoosh. She approached the lone chair and sat down on it.

"Hello Alexa."

"Hello Lexi." Her own face appeared on the screen.

"I miss you." Lexi said, smiling at her.

"I miss you too," Alexa said, "but it is better this way for you."

"You will always be my supercomputer self, Alexa. I love you."

The AI smiled. "Do you think El has a purpose for me too? I feel a bit lost as if I'm only a machine now."

Lexi gazed at her, "I think He has a purpose with everything in creation. Every atom and particle contains life and can react to His love. You are loved, too, Alexa and exist with the purpose to live for Him."

"Thank you."

Lexi grinned. "I have a surprise for you. Dad installed a nano-micro receiver and sender into my ear almost like the one he had when he was in prison. If I activate it, I can talk to you and you to me anytime."

Alexa chortled. "Do you think I didn't know that? But I'm delighted he did. I'm yours after all."

Lexi blew a kiss to the screens and stood up. "Time for us to go change the world for the better."

Thank you for reading Alexa. I hope you enjoyed the story as much as I did writing it.

Please leave a review for me on Facebook, Amazon and Goodreads.

Reviews bring books to people's attention and help the story reach more people.

Thank you for your help!

About The Author

Clara Berge is a South African-born author who lives in England. Besides being a dreamer, she is the wife of an amazing man, mother of five wonderful children, and the keeper of her home. Disclaimer - Her stories are sometimes born between piles of laundry.

Contact her at clara@claraberge.com

www.claraberge.com

https://www.goodreads.com/author/show/18288319.Clara_Berge

https://www.facebook.com/writingwithheaven

Seraph Creative is a collective of artists, writers, theologians & illustrators who desire to see the body of Christ grow into full maturity, walking in their inheritance as Sons Of God on the Earth.

Sign up to our newsletter to know about the release of the next book in the series, as well as other exciting releases.

Visit our website:
www.seraphcreative.org